Deck the Heart

Also By

Nicole Mullaney

Other books written by Nicole Mullaney include:

Ivy & Mistletoe
The Maltese Holiday
Magic in Mount Holly (coming soon)

Books Written by Character Ethan Dulane
Ethan Dulane is a Character Created by Candy Cain &
Nicole Mullaney for Joy & Hope

Joy & Hope

For Adult Romance Check out Nikki A Lamers

<u>The Unforgettable Series:</u>
The Unforgettable Summer
Unforgettable Nights
Unforgettable Dreams
Unforgettable Memories
The Unforgettable One
Unforgettable Mistakes (Coming 2021)

<u>The Home Duet:</u>
Dreams Lost and Found
Finding Home

Deck the Heart

By Nicole Mullaney

Based on the Screenplay written by Candy Cain

Table of Contents

Copyright

Dedication

For our boys,
Tyler and Charles,
who decked our own hearts
before we even met them.

Chapter 1

Chris

I lower myself into my black leather office chair behind my black, L-shaped desk, and pull up my calendar on the computer to verify the time of my next phone call. I run my hand through my short golden blond hair, brushing it to the right and off my forehead, as I reach for the office phone.

I pick up the phone and dial in for my scheduled call. A woman answers, as I'm glancing through the information I need for this call, "This is June, may I help you?"

"Yes, This is Chris Ackerman. I have a call scheduled with Mr. Vincent," I inform her.

"Of course, Mr. Ackerman," she acknowledges. "Would you mind holding for just a moment, please?" she requests.

"Yes, I'll hold," I reply automatically. I lean back in my cushioned chair, while I wait for him to pick up.

My intercom buzzes and I push up towards my desk and press the button to answer my assistant. "I'm on hold, Beth," I advise.

"But," she begins, attempting to tell me what she needs, but I press the button to disconnect before she continues. I don't want to miss my client and have to reschedule.

The intercom buzzes again, almost immediately. I push the button to respond to Beth. "Not now!" I insist. I disconnect the intercom, holding the office phone to my ear, still on hold and waiting for Mr. Vincent.

Out of the corner of my eye, I notice as Beth steps into my office. She's about 5'7" and lean with straight, shoulder length, platinum blonde hair and bright blue eyes. She has been my assistant for nearly five years now and she knows me quite well. She's always on top of everything, from being efficient, detailed, hard working and honest, to being dressed professionally, just like she is today. She's wearing a slim, knee length black skirt and a jade green silk blouse with simple black pumps. "Mr. Ackerman?" she requests.

"I'm on the phone," I reiterate, in case she didn't hear me on the intercom.

She grimaces and acknowledges, "I know." She hesitates before adding, "Your mother has called eleven times this morning."

My eyes widen in surprise. For clarification I repeat, "Eleven?"

She pinches her lips tightly together and nods her head slowly in confirmation. Then she reiterates, "Eleven. She said it's an emergency and needs to talk to you," she enlightens me.

My stomach flips anxiously at the word, emergency. Last time she called for an emergency it wasn't good news. "About?" I question.

She purses her lips and shrugs her shoulders, knowing I won't like her answer. "I don't know," she concedes.

I sigh heavily in resignation. "Fine," I grumble. "Put her through," I concede, as my heartbeat instantly picks up its pace. I hope everything is okay. I'm 32, but we've been through a lot lately and my mom saying there's an emergency puts my nerves on edge. "Pick up line one for me and reschedule that call when they finally pick up," I request.

"Yes sir," she acknowledges.

9

She walks out of the room and I press a button to place my current call on hold and wait for Beth to send my mom through. My mom is a beautiful woman with long, thick, golden blonde hair, soft blue eyes and she's almost six inches shorter than my five feet and eleven inches. I've been told many times how much I look like her with the same hair and eyes. The phone rings almost instantly. I pick it up and grasp the receiver tightly in my hand, my anxiety immediately rising, no matter what I try to tell myself. "Mom? What's wrong?" I demand, without preamble.

"Is that any way to greet your mother?" she prompts, casually.

"Mom!" I call, attempting to bring her attention back to the reason she needed to speak with me right away. "Are you okay? What's the emergency?" I question.

"The emergency is that I haven't heard from my only son in nearly a week," she announces, sounding slightly disappointed in me.

I close my eyes and breathe a sigh of relief, as I run my free hand through my hair. "Mom, I'm sorry," I apologize and open my eyes. "It's a busy time of year," I remind her.

"You should never be too busy for your family, Christian," she emphasizes, scolding me.

I wince as a wave of guilt washes over me. She shouldn't have to remind me of that, especially after going through so much the last couple months. I guess sometimes it's just easier not to think about it all. I sigh heavily and quietly admit, "I know. You're right." I pause and attempt to start this conversation over. "It's nice to hear your voice, Mom," I convey, truthfully.

"That's more like it," she declares. "How are you, Honey?" she probes.

"Busy. Really busy," I answer, honestly. "We're going from Black Friday right into our holiday campaign," I inform her.

"That's not what I meant," she claims. "How are you?" she repeats, her tone a little softer to communicate her intentions.

I pause and take a deep breath as a wave of sadness washes over me. "I'm okay. I really miss Grandpa, so I've been throwing myself into my work," I confess. I swallow hard, fighting the sudden lump in my throat. "I keep picking up the phone to call him," I admit.

I hear the sadness and empathy in her voice as she continues, "So do I, Baby." She sighs and then takes a deep breath. "Which is why I'm calling," she reveals.

"Really? What's up?" I prompt.

"Well, today was the reading of Grandpa's will," she reminds me.

"Oh, that's right," I acknowledge. "He split everything between you, Aunt Jean and Uncle Jack, right?" I question.

"Almost," she replies. "He left some special items for all of the grandkids," she discloses.

"Really?" I prompt, surprised.

"Yes," she confirms. "Emma got his pocket watch and some of Grandma's jewelry. Jack Jr. got his car. Clint got the boat. He opened some small trust funds for the younger ones," she informs me. "And you, well," she begins and trails off, like she's not quite sure what to say.

"It's okay, Mom," I tell her, attempting to comfort her. "I don't need anything," I claim.

"Chris, you were his favorite," she proclaims.

I chuckle softly and my heart clenches, as memories of him run through my mind. "Yeah, I know," I concede.

11

"Chris," she pauses, "he left you the house," she states.

I gasp and my eyes widen in surprise. "In Maine?" I question, needing clarification.

"Yes," she confirms.

"Really?" I prod.

"Yes," she reiterates. "His attorney is going to contact you," she notifies me.

"I can't believe this!" I mumble, leaning back in my chair in shock. I spin around and let my head fall back as I look at the picture on the wall behind my desk. It's an image of a rough ocean, near a rocky shore, looking as if the sun is shining down on all of it. It not only helps push me forward during tough times like this, showing the light in the midst of a storm. It also always reminds me of the coast near the house there. "I love that house," I assert.

"Chris, there's a stipulation," she adds.

I flinch, hoping it's something I can handle. "A stipulation?" I inquire.

"Yes. In order for you to get the house, you have to host Christmas this year, just like Grandpa always did," she enlightens me. My mouth drops open in shock. How am I supposed to do that so quickly and from so far away? I still have my job to think about too. "Chris? Are you there, Honey?" she prompts, pulling me out of my thoughts.

"Yeah," I mumble. "I'm here, Mom. Just surprised is all."

"I know you're busy, Honey, but..." she begins and trails off.

"I'll find a way," I insist, resolved to figure it out. If it meant that much to Grandpa, there's no way I would ever say no. I would do anything for him. Besides, I would never take a chance of losing that house. It means too much to our family...to me. I have so many memories there, especially with him. I'm not giving that away for anything.

"Are you sure?" she prompts.

"Absolutely. Grandpa wanted it this way. I'll figure it out," I proclaim. I'm determined to do things exactly as he wanted them.

"Christmas is less than a month away," she reminds me.

"I know," I acknowledge. "I'm on it, Mom," I maintain. I have to be. There's no other option.

"Okay," she acknowledges. "Let me know if you need any help."

"I will," I agree.

"Love you," she murmurs.

"Love you too, Mom," I reply.

"Bye," she adds.

"Goodbye," I respond. Then, I hang up the phone and return it to the cradle.

"There's no time like the present," I mumble to myself. I stand up from my desk and walk towards Beth's desk in reception. She sits in a high-back, black, rolling chair behind a tall, dark pine, two-tiered desk, with a black granite top. Her office is located just down the hall from mine and on the other side, it leads towards the rest of the offices, including my boss, Larry Link. She's sitting at her computer, typing as I approach. I lean on her desk to get her attention. She almost immediately stops what she's doing and looks up at me, giving me her full attention.

"Yes, Mr. Ackerman?" she inquires.

"Is Larry around?" I ask.

"Yes," she confirms. "Mr. Link just returned from lunch," she enlightens me.

"Great," I mumble. "Let him know I'm on my way up, please," I request.

She nods in acknowledgement, "Yes, Sir."

"Thanks," I murmur, appreciatively.

I knock on her desk twice and step away as Beth picks up the phone to call him. I take my time walking down the hallway, making sure to give her time to notify him I'm on my way. At the same time, I run over what I need to say to him in my head. I step up to Larry's open door and knock, alerting him of my presence. He glances up from his desk, containing nothing but his coffee, his office phone, a newspaper and the monitor and keyboard for his computer, with a printer off to the side. Behind him there's a brick wall, with a large window, overlooking the city. "Chris," he acknowledges. "Come in," he instructs, waving me inside.

"Thanks," I reply.

Larry is about the same age as my parents and about two inches shorter than me. He's balding on top, with gray hair in the back and on the sides. He has brown eyes and a friendly smile, when you can pull a smile from him, but he's extremely focused on his work. I lower myself into a black leather chair opposite him, prepared to jump right in.

"Did you have a nice Thanksgiving," he questions, the moment I sit down, before I have a chance to say a word.

I nod my head in confirmation. "I did, thanks. Watched the parade, had dinner," I explain, vaguely. "You?" I prompt, politely.

"It was great," he claims, happily. "Thanksgiving is my favorite holiday. Being around the family is good for us," he asserts.

14

I force a smile and admit, "This year was just me. We had my grandfather's funeral a couple weeks ago and I had a lot to catch up on."

"You should have joined me and Loretta. There's nothing like a Link family Thanksgiving," he claims.

I smile, grateful for the offer. "Thanks. I appreciate that," I murmur. "There was just too much to do for Black Friday," I maintain.

"You did a great job too, Chris," he praises. "I'm going through the numbers and sales are up seventeen percent from last year."

I wince, as a feeling of disappointment washes over me. "Is that all?" I prod.

"That's all?!" he exclaims, wide eyed. "We set our goal for an increase of five percent," he reminds me. "You knocked it out of the park!" he emphasizes.

"I was hoping for twenty," I concede.

"Twenty?" he probes, with a small smile on his face. "You're a machine. You need to take some time off," he suggests.

I jump at the opportunity and mumble, "Funny you should say that." I chuckle and rub the back of my neck nervously.

"Uh-oh," he grumbles, his demeanor suddenly changing. He stares me down momentarily, making me even more anxious. "You're not leaving me for the holidays are you?" he inquires.

I shake my head and mumble, "Not exactly." His eyes widen with my response and I quickly explain the situation. "My grandfather left me his house in Maine and I have to host Christmas up there. Do you mind if I work remotely until New Year's Eve?" I propose. "I'll start the New Year fresh in my office," I add.

A look of relief crosses his face. "You don't have to come back exactly on New Year's Day," he offers.

I paste a grateful smile on my face and mumble, "Well, we'll see."

"Whatever you need to do, Chris," he claims. "Just keep up the good work," he encourages.

"Thanks, Larry," I reply, appreciatively. "Merry Christmas," I add. I stand up and take a step towards his desk, holding my hand out in gratitude.

He clasps my hand and shakes. "You too," he replies.

I release his hand and turn around. I step out of his office and quickly make my way back towards Beth in reception. The moment she sees me, she stands up and holds out a small stack of phone messages for me. "Mr. Ackerman, I have a few messages for you. Mr. Carter called," she begins.

I take the phone messages from her, but hold my hand up to stop her from continuing. "Don't worry about it, Beth. Do me a favor and reschedule all of my phone calls for the rest of today and tomorrow to Wednesday," I advise.

"Yes, Sir," she immediately responds.

"And get me a list of the five best event planners and decorators in Christmas Cove, Maine," I instruct.

Her eyebrows draw down in confusion and she questions, "Christmas Cove?"

"Well, South Bristol, actually. My house is in Christmas Cove," I elaborate.

She looks even more puzzled. "I'm sorry, Mr. Ackerman, but you're confusing me. You have a house in Maine?" she asks for clarification.

I nod my head and acknowledge, "Apparently. It's a long story," I add, waving off an explanation for the moment. "Get me the list, reschedule my appointments and then you can have the rest of the day off," I inform her.

Her eyes widen in surprise as she smiles up at me. "Really?" she prompts.

I nod my head in confirmation, "Yes and come in around eleven tomorrow. I'll be telecommuting until the New Year."

Her mouth drops open and she stands frozen, appearing momentarily stunned. "I don't know what to say," she finally mumbles.

"Yeah, well, neither do I, Beth," I stammer. "It's all a bit sudden" I concur. "Just get me that info, will you, please?" I repeat.

"Yes, Sir," she agrees.

"And reschedule my calls," I reiterate.

"Absolutely," she confirms.

I force a small smile and appreciatively mumble, "Thank you." She returns my smile and nods in acknowledgement, as I turn and stride back for my office. I have to tie up all the loose ends I can in the next couple hours and make sure I'm prepared to work remotely. I don't want to forget anything.

Chapter 2

Chris

I continue carrying filled boxes from my apartment, downstairs and out to my car in the parking garage. I pass by my best friend, Jordan Pike, doing the same. Like me, he's dressed comfortably in blue jeans, a thick, gray, ribbed sweater and sneakers. Jordan towers over me at six feet, six inches. He's a good-looking man with a fantastic sense of humor and an even bigger heart. He has light chocolate brown skin, black hair, cut close to his scalp and coffee brown eyes. We met in college and started rooming together our sophomore year. We had a couple other close friends that roomed with us when we moved to an apartment off campus our last two years, but Jordan has always been like a brother to me. We have a great time together and we will forever have each other's backs. We've been best friends for a long time, nearly since the day we met. I couldn't ask for a better friend and I wouldn't want to.

I load the boxes I'm carrying into the back of my navy blue SUV and close the tailgate. Then I step back and brush the dust off my tan and white button down and black lined winter coat. I make my way out of the dark, cement parking garage and back upstairs. I return to my apartment to find Jordan standing in the middle of the living room, looking around. "I'm just checking to make sure I didn't miss any boxes or bags," he murmurs. "I think this is it," he declares, gesturing towards two large black suitcases and one navy blue one, along with a three-foot cardboard tube filled with a few charts from work.

"That's great," I vocalize. I scan the room as well, knowing I brought everything I want to take with me to this room. "I believe you're right. Let's just grab all of this then and I guess I'll head out," I inform him. We both walk over to the last of my things and pick everything up, rolling the suitcases. Then we stride through the front door and I set the suitcases down to pull the door closed behind us. I quickly lock my door, before we make our way down the short hallway to catch the elevator to return downstairs.

Jordan pushes the button for the elevator and I breathe a sigh of relief when the doors slide open immediately. I need to get on the road soon, or I'll be too tired to make it all the way there. We step inside the small space, hauling all of my things along with us. I set my suitcase down and push the button for the parking garage. We both lean casually against the back of the elevator, as we start to descend. "I can't thank you enough, Jordan. I greatly appreciate you coming over to help me out today," I express, emphatically.

He nods his head in acknowledgement and grins wide, "No, problem. I know you'd do the same for me."

I chuckle and nod in agreement. "You know I would," I concur. The elevator stops and the stainless steel doors slide open. I nod my head towards Jordan and he walks out first, while I follow along behind him. Jordan backs into the glass door leading to the garage, pushing it open and pauses, allowing me to step through. I walk to the back of my car and open the tailgate again. He loads the navy blue suitcase and the cardboard tube into the back, first. Then I lift the last two suitcases and place them inside.

"You sure you're only going for a month?" he prompts. He arches his eyebrows in challenge, as the corners of his mouth twitch up in amusement. "It seems like you're moving with all this stuff you have," he teases, making me chuckle.

I step back and nod in acknowledgement. I know where he's coming from, but I have a lot to do while I'm there. "I have to move my entire life up to Maine for the next month, Jordan. I don't want to chance leaving anything behind," I claim.

"Why don't you just fly up there?" he inquires.

"Because I'll need my car. It's not like New York, where we can walk everywhere," I attempt to explain. Although truthfully, unless you go up there, even if it's just for a visit, it's extremely difficult to understand what life in Maine is really like.

"Cabs?" he prods.

I huff a laugh and shake my head in response. "No, man. I'm in the middle of nowhere," I emphasize. Cabs do exist there, but at times it could take forever waiting for one to pick you up.

"Is the town really called 'Christmas Cove'?" he prompts.

I shrug my shoulders and mumble, "Kind of. It's on Rutherford Island in South Bristol. The story is that John Smith harbored his boat there during Christmas in the 1600's and gave it that name," I explain.

"John Smith?" he questions. He arches his eyebrows in surprise and probes, "The Pocahontas guy?"

I can't help, but laugh at his description and nod my head in response. "Yeah, him," I confirm. "The town is still south of Bristol, but Christmas Cove is a real place. There are only a handful of homes there," I elaborate.

Jordan grins and proclaims, "And your grandfather had one of those homes."

I nod my head in confirmation, "Exactly. My grandma and grandpa bought it from his father and passed it down to me."

His grin widens and he announces, "No mortgage. Sweet."

"It's beyond that, Jordan. All of my family's Christmas memories are there. My mom grew up in that house. Everyone goes to the lake house for Christmas. We didn't know what we were going to do for this Christmas since Grandpa died," I elaborate, thinking about my parents, aunts, uncles and cousins. I gulp down the sudden lump in my throat as I fight to keep my emotions at bay with every little bit I reveal.

He smiles sadly and nods his head in understanding. "Looks like he decided for you," he murmurs.

I force a smile and nod my head slowly. I take a deep breath and cautiously exhale, attempting to calm my pounding heart. I need to change the subject. "Why don't you come up with your folks?" I suggest.

Jordan's mouth drops open and his eyes widen in surprise. "For Christmas?" he asks for clarification.

I shrug and offer him a genuine smile. "Yeah. Why not?"

"I don't know. I'll talk to them about it. My sister is spending Christmas at her new in-laws house in Utah, so it was just going to be the three of us anyway," he informs me, with a shrug of his shoulders, acting as if it's no big deal.

"Well, maybe this would be a good distraction for them," I advocate. I'm sure they're having a difficult time not having her home for the holidays for the very first time. "It's not such a bad drive from Boston for them," I insist.

"Maybe. I'll talk to them," he declares. "Who else will be there?" he questions.

I give my head a light shake and the corners of my mouth curve upwards, just thinking about family

Christmases at that house. "Man, my entire family," I mumble, reverently. "Mom and dad, my two aunts and uncles, at least three of my cousins," I begin, listing everyone I know will definitely be there.

Jordan's eyes widen in surprise and he declares, "That's a full house. You sure you want three more?" he challenges.

"Sure," I insist, nodding my head in confirmation. "It's Christmas and it's a big house," I emphasize.

He arches his eyebrows in question and asks, "How big?"

I chuckle softly and demand, "Come for Christmas and find out."

He laughs at my response. "I'll talk to my folks," he reiterates. "I promise. But how are you going to pull all this together?" he questions, with a slight grimace.

I don't blame him for wondering. It's a lot to take on for anyone. I smirk and murmur mysteriously, "I have my ways." He chuckles and shakes his head in amusement, as I turn and slam my trunk closed. "Okay, I need to head out," I acknowledge, with a resigned sigh. "Traffic is going to start getting heavy in a little bit," I inform him, realizing it's almost rush hour.

He grimaces and nods his head in understanding. "How long will it take for you to get there, anyway?" he prods, curiously.

"About seven hours," I divulge.

"Not bad," he shrugs.

"Not at all," I concur. "You should make the drive," I reiterate.

He chuckles in response. "I get the hint, Chris," he emphasizes. "I'll do what I can. Have a safe trip," he expresses.

"Thanks," I acknowledge. "For everything," I stress. I step towards him and hold out my arms, in appreciation. He meets me halfway and we give each other a quick hug, with a hard pat on the back. I release him and step away. I offer him a small wave, as I walk around to the driver's side of the car. I open the door and slip in behind the wheel, pulling the door closed behind me. I relax into my tan leather seats and reach up, grabbing my seatbelt, pulling it across my chest and buckling it with a click. Then I put my foot on the brake and push the button to start the car. I roll down the window and put the car in reverse before I slowly start to back out of my assigned parking spot. I put the car in drive and put my hand out the window to wave to Jordan as I leave.

"See you later!" he calls out.

I smile to myself as I pull away from my building and onto the road, turning towards the highway. I quickly roll up the window, feeling a chill in the air. Then I turn on the radio and a Christmas song instantly starts jingling through the speakers. I listen as I drive north, thinking about everything I have to get done for Christmas. I hope I'm able to find someone who can help out at this late of date. There's no way I could handle all of it on my own. As I make it past the city, through Connecticut and past the Boston area, the traffic on the roads finally begins letting up. I pass briefly through New Hampshire before I reach the Maine Bridge, or the Piscataqua River Bridge. It's a through arch bridge, separating the two states and a landmark for me, although I still have about two hours to go. I smile to myself as I reach the border, right in the middle of the bridge.

I remain in the right lane and slow down just a little bit as I pass a cobalt blue sign stating, "Maine" in large block letters. Just underneath Maine, the sign announces, "Welcome Home" with the final line, the familiar slogan, "The way life should be." I roll down my window a little bit and take a deep breath, inhaling the scent of the fresh air, heavy with pine. I love that smell. That scent alone is one thing that always reminds me of Maine, Christmas and most importantly, my grandfather. A lump forms in my throat and a tingly ache spreads throughout my insides, almost instantly. I quickly roll up the window, the wind and cold air, suddenly too much to handle.

I take a deep breath and exhale slowly as I step on the gas, picking up my previous pace. It's been a really long day between work, rearranging my schedule with Beth, packing and this long drive. I just want to get there. Although, I'll admit to myself that I'm a little anxious about what it's going to be like walking into the house tonight. This will be the first time without him. I take one more deep breath and readjust in my seat, as I turn up the radio, drowning out my thoughts in the light sounds of the music.

I exit off the highway onto US-1 near Brunswick, thankful I'm finally close. At least traffic will be much slower as I make my way through many of the quaint coastal towns. I leave Bath, passing by a Navy ship docked at the Bath Iron Works Shipyard, just before I cross over the Kennebec River. I drive through Wiscasset, the antique shops all closed for the night and no line outside of the closed up red and white shack of Red's Eats for their famous lobster rolls. Any time they're open, there is almost always a line curved around the block. I cross over the Sheepscot River, with Red's in my rearview mirror and drive a few more miles before I spot my exit. I turn off and drive through Main Street in Damariscotta, before veering off to the right on the other end of town, heading towards South Bristol. I finally cross over onto Rutherford Island and breathe a sigh of relief.

The closer I come to Christmas Cove, the more the hilly country roads begin to twist and turn. I slow down, searching for the entrance to the driveway between the trees. My headlights are the only lights around, with the clouds in the sky blocking the moon and the stars at the moment. I finally pull into the long, gravel driveway at my grandfather's house, surrounded by trees on both sides, separating the large properties. Well, I guess it's my house now. I attempt to gulp down the lump in my throat, barely able to even make out the outline of the house without any light. I put the car in park next to the garage and turn it off with a heavy sigh. "I'm here," I murmur, softly. I unbuckle my seatbelt, suddenly overwhelmed with emotions and nervous to walk inside.

Chapter 3

Meredith

I stand at the back of the room, just before the South Bristol Chamber of Commerce meeting is about to start. I glance down at my outfit, starting at my short, black, velvet boots with a two-inch heel, adding some height to my petite five feet four inch frame. Then I move up to my long, black, pencil skirt with thin, vertical white stripes, brushing off an imaginary piece of lint, before nervously running my hands over my cranberry colored thin sweater with a lightly ruffled hem and one-inch decorative lace along the V-neck at the top. I take a deep breath and exhale slowly, trying to calm my anxiety as my stomach twists into knots.

I smile and nod politely to the two woman walking by me and making their way to a seat. I guess I should do the same. I walk slowly down the middle of the room, with the rows of chairs splitting the room into two sides, breaking up the room with a tall, oak podium at the front, right in the center. I find an empty seat in a chair with a black slipcover to my left, towards the front of the room. I don't like having the spotlight on me, especially in front of such an obviously successful group of people like this, but I need to be here to help get my business off the ground and my business is important to me. Plus, I want to be here to support the community as a business owner. I feel like it's not only a responsibility, but also a privilege and I'm proud to do my part. Of course the hard part is keeping my nerves under control.

I look around the room, trying to keep my mind occupied, until the meeting begins. The room itself reminds me of a classroom with its white tile floors and cream walls. The Christmas decorations as well as posters and banners of local businesses, add much needed color around the room. Glittery white and blue snowflakes hang from the ceiling and an eight-foot Christmas tree stands in the corner. It's strung with white lights, decorated with red, gold and silver ornaments and topped off with an angel, shining brightly. Several local businesses have their poster hung in the front behind the podium, on their own banner stand, or in the back by the refreshment table. The banners at the front include Matthews Brothers windows, Cellar Door Winery, North Country Wind Bells, Pro 31 Cleaning Solutions, King Eider's Pub, Shannon's Unshelled, making me hungry for lobster, Q-Team Tree Service, Dow Furniture and an area Discovery map attached to the front of the podium. I'm impressed by the variety of business advertising at this meeting.

My brown eyes roam over all the men and women spread out around the room. I'm pleased to find there are a wide variety of people of all ages here and all dressed professionally. A tall, thin woman with wavy, shoulder length blonde hair and blue eyes steps up to the podium and gets the meeting started. She's wearing a navy blue pantsuit with a white, silk top underneath, accessorized with navy blue pumps and a string of pearls wrapped around her neck. The way she holds herself and the way she speaks practically screams power. She calls the meeting to order and introduces herself, "For those of you who don't know me, I'm Felicia Johnson. We have a lot to cover tonight, so I'm going to jump right in to the agenda."

I listen to all old business, attempting to grasp the kinds of things that are happening in the community, but even with living here for so long, it seems like it might take time to keep up with it all. It feels like almost no time has passed when Felicia smiles and broadcasts, "And now for new business. The South Bristol Chamber of Commerce has a new member. I'd like us all to give a warm welcome to Meredith Block, the proud owner of Merry Events." She gestures in my direction and I smile and timidly wave to everyone in the room. With all eyes suddenly focused on me as they clap loudly, I feel my face heat in embarrassment. "Why don't you come up here and tell us a little bit about your business, Meredith?" she suggests.

I feel my face turn an even deeper shade of red. I point to myself and arch my eyebrows in question. "Me?" I prompt.

"Of course," she confirms. "Any small business owner is their best advocate," she advises. I hear the crowd murmur their agreement and I attempt to gulp down the sudden lump in my throat. "Don't be shy, Meredith," she encourages. "You might just have a client or two sitting in this group," she reminds me. She's right. Business owners can also be each other's best advocates.

I stand up slowly, pulling my long, brown, wavy hair protectively over my shoulder as I reluctantly concede. "Yeah, I guess," I mumble.

"You shouldn't guess, Meredith. You're a business owner. You need to exude confidence," she claims. "Let's give her some encouragement!" she requests, turning towards the rest of the room. She starts clapping and everyone else in the room soon follows her lead. I cautiously make my way to the front of the room, not wanting to fall before I get there.

The applause quiets down and I force a smile as I turn to her. I take a deep breath as my heart begins to race. "Thank you Felicia," I murmur.

"You're welcome," she replies, smiling broadly. She takes a step back, allowing me to step in front of the podium. When I don't move, she nods her head at me, encouraging me to begin.

I take a deep shaky breath, attempting to control my anxiety, as I force myself to step in front of the podium. I clear my throat and place my sweaty hands on top of the podium for support. "Hi! I'm Merry Block. That's short for Meredith. I mean, Merry is, not Block. Block is my last name," I stammer, awkwardly.

I look over at Felicia, almost pleading, as my face suddenly turns a deep shade of red and my eyes widen to the size of saucers. I'm terrible at talking in front groups of people. She waves her arm towards me and smiles. "Go on," she prods.

I take another deep breath and exhale slowly. I can do this, I tell myself, hoping it's the truth. "I just opened my company, Merry Events. I plan events, decorate and cook for small parties," I begin.

"Are you licensed?" Felicia interrupts.

"What?" I ask. I'm not sure what she just said. It's hard to hear over the rush of the blood pounding in my ears.

"Are you licensed to work food service in Maine?" she elaborates.

"Oh!" I exclaim, understanding her question. "Yes, of course. Licensed, bonded and insured," I declare. Realizing I left something out, I quickly add, "And trained! Classically trained in the culinary arts. I did a year abroad in Paris, actually, so I really do know how to cook," I claim.

"Why event planning?" Felicia prompts.

"Well, I really enjoy planning parties and decorating. I'm the hostess with the mostest, I guess," I proclaim. I shrug my shoulders and paste a smile on my face, as I laugh nervously at myself.

"Why did you decide to open your business now?" Felicia prompts. "The winter is such a difficult time to start a new business," she adds, as explanation for her question.

"Well, I've always been planning parties. My parents never really got into birthdays or the holidays or anything, so I was always left up to my own devices for them," I elaborate, revealing more than I intended in my explanation.

Felicia's eyes fill with sympathy as she meets my gaze. "That's so sad," she mumbles. Sounds of agreement and empathy come from the crowd, causing me to panic.

"Oh, no!" I plead and shake my head, as my eyes widen again, almost desperate. "No, not at all," I emphasize. "My mom is a neurosurgeon and my dad is a scientist. They were just really busy and didn't find the holidays important. I really loved planning them so that we could do things together," I attempt to defend my family. I gulp down the lump in my throat and fight a grimace before admitting, "Even if it was only a couple times during the year."

"You don't spend the holidays with them?" Felicia clarifies, in surprise.

I push my shoulders back, feigning the confidence I don't feel. "No, not really. I hosted "Friendsgiving" this year at my house and I hope to get a Christmas client," I explain.

"A Christmas client?" Felicia repeats.

A man in the front row raises his hand, bringing all eyes to him. He's a good-looking man with naturally tanned skin, a round face with a closely trimmed beard, black hair and brown eyes, wearing black pants and shoes, with a white button down dress shirt and a dusty blue sport coat. He immediately lowers his hand and inquires, "What's a Christmas client?"

I nod my head and explain, "A Christmas client is someone that doesn't have the time to decorate for Christmas and lets me plan, decorate and cook for their celebration."

"Then where will you spend it?" Felicia questions, sounding concerned.

I wince and feel my cheeks turn pink in embarrassment. "That really doesn't have anything to do with my business," I stammer. Plus, it's not a question I want to answer in front of a group of strangers and business owners around the community. I want people to view me the same way they do everyone else.

She nods in agreement. "You're right. I'm sorry. I didn't mean to get personal," she acknowledges.

I force myself to smile and insist, "It's fine! It's fine. Really. I have plenty of friends in South Bristol and no shortage of invitations for Christmas," I blurt out, uncomfortably. I feel my face heat even more. I'm sure it matches the color of my shirt by now. I laugh nervously, attempting to brush it off.

Felicia nods and prompts, "In conclusion..."

I nod my head in acknowledgement. "Right. In conclusion, I'm able to help you with any celebration and turn it into a Merry Event," I announce with fake cheer. "Thank you," I proclaim. I feel my shoulders relax, feeling both relieved and grateful for the opportunity, as I step away from the podium. Everyone around the room claps for me, as I quickly make my way back to my seat.

I sit down just as Felicia continues the meeting. "You'll find the information for Merry Events on the back of your agenda. Our next order of business is the South Bristol New Year's Eve Party, sponsored by John LaRue at King Eider's Pub. John?" she requests.

Everyone cheers as John rises. He's a tall, older man with thick, gray hair and blue eyes. I watch as he walks to the front in his black suit, with a blue and green striped tie. I breathe another sigh of relief, knowing the focus is really off of me.

About fifteen minutes later, the meeting is adjourned and everyone rises and begins talking and laughing with one another. I make my way to the back of the room, near the refreshment table, covered with cookies, pastries, cake, water, soda, coffee and tea. I look up at the banners above the table, one is for The Bradley Inn and the other is for the Botanical Gardens, advertising their display of holiday lights with a moose made of flowers. He's made up of mostly purple, accented with a little blue and has antlers in bright yellow. I smile up at the beautiful image.

"Good job tonight," Felicia announces, stepping up behind me.

I spin around to face her and smile. "Hardly," I acknowledge.

"No, really," she insists. "I put you on the spot and you handled yourself well."

I look up at her, unsure if that's true. "You think so?" I question.

She nods in confirmation and mumbles, "Sure." She pauses and proclaims, "You could be more confident, but you'll get there."

I laugh at her honesty. She's definitely right. I grimace and admit, "I hate speaking in front of crowds."

She shrugs and concedes, "So do I."

My eyes widen in surprise. "Really?" I prod. "You're such a natural at it," I praise her.

She laughs in response and shakes her head in denial. "Oh, no I'm not. I have to hype myself up for these things," she confesses.

"But you have people eating out of the palm of your hand," I claim.

She waves off my comment and mumbles, "Hardly." I look at her, the corners of my mouth tugging upwards, realizing she repeated the same thing I said earlier. Her eyes sparkle and she releases a laugh, causing me to relax and laugh along with her. "I like you," she declares.

"Thanks," I acknowledge. "You're not so bad yourself," I add.

"I'm going to give you a lead," she announces.

"A lead?" I prompt. My heart takes off with excitement at the possibility.

She nods her head in confirmation, "Yes. Here," she offers. She reaches into her black purse, slung over her shoulder and fishes out a slip of paper. She holds it out to me between her fingers.

"What's that?" I inquire.

"A woman called me today and said that her boss just inherited a home in Christmas Cove and he needs to host a big family Christmas," she explains.

I feel myself stand a little taller as I ask, "Really?"

She nods her head and confirms, "Yes. She is looking for an event planner to plan, decorate and cook."

I smile broadly and broadcast with eagerness, "That's right up my alley!"

She nods in agreement, "I know. I knew you were coming tonight, but I wanted to see how you handled yourself," she informs me.

My eyebrows draw down in confusion and I question, "You tested me?"

"Well, I had to do something. I don't usually give referrals for people that I don't know," she insists.

I nod my head in understanding. "You won't regret it, Felicia," I claim. "I promise." I take the slip of paper from her, feeling my excitement building up inside of me.

"I know I won't," she acknowledges. "Please call tonight before eleven," she instructs. "Have a Merry Christmas, Meredith."

"Merry Christmas?" I challenge. "We've got a few weeks until Christmas," I remind her.

She grins broadly and emphatically informs me, "Honey, it's supposed to start snowing really bad and I am not a fan of the cold."

My eyes widen in surprise. "But you live in Maine," I reiterate.

She grimaces and nods in acknowledgement. "I know. My husband wanted to live here, so we made a deal. Every year, we go to the Bahamas for a month over the holidays," she enlightens me.

"Oh," I murmur, dragging out the word. "That sounds really nice," I concede.

She smiles reverently and agrees, "Trust me, it is."

"Thank you so much, Felicia. Really," I emphasize.

I hold out my hand to thank her and she smiles warmly at me. "Give me a hug," she announces and holds out her arms to me. I meet her halfway and hug her, grateful. "Let's share that girl power," she adds.

I grin and proclaim, "Girl power is right." I'm thrilled she is giving me this opportunity. Hopefully, this will be exactly what I need. Now I just have to get the job.

Chapter 4

Meredith

I pull in the driveway of my modest cape style home. It's a pale yellow house, with black shutters, roof and front door. I have a small flower garden in front of the house on each side of my front walkway, but this time of year the only thing left is a row of green holly bushes I have decorated with white lights. The walkway is lined with large, red and white candy canes, three on each side. I step up onto my front porch, the pole and railing wrapped with thick garland and white lights, enhanced with a large wreath decorated with pinecones and a red and green gingham ribbon, woven through the greens, hanging off the front of the rail facing the street. I unlock the front door, adorned with a large wreath decorated with a thick, red velvet ribbon tied in an elaborate bow, along with red ornaments and small silver and gold balls.

I pocket my keys and push the door open. I step inside and immediately call for my cat as I wipe my feet on the Santa rug just inside the door. "Thaddeus! I'm home!" I announce. I close the door behind me and take off my coat. I open the door just to my right, reaching for a hanger. I slip my coat over it and hang it up and instantly close the door. The flat, red and green, wire ornament, bounces against the back of the door as it clicks shut. I set my purse down next to a wooden Merry Christmas sign sitting on top of my wine rack, underneath the front windows. Then, I squat down and reach for the black cord on the ground and grasp it, plugging it into the wall and lighting up my seven and a half foot Christmas tree standing in the corner. I decorated my tree with white lights, and all kinds of colorful ornaments.

I stand up and pick up my purse, taking it with me as I walk between a long accent table, backed up against the stairs and the back of my L-shaped, chocolate brown couch. The table has a wood bottom painted black and a marble black and gray-checkered top, decorated with a stuffed snowman, a Santa snow globe and a Christmas tin, along with a few ornaments I want to add to the Christmas tree later on. I put accent pillows on the couch, including one with a snowman, another with a penguin couple and a third with a large red poinsettia flower. Across from the couch I have a flat screen television mounted up above the tan tiled fireplace accented with a beautiful ivory mantle and surround. I placed red and white Christmas candles atop the mantle with a red and white Christmas stocking hanging on each end, one for me and one for Thaddeus.

I wander past my half bath on my left and the basement stairs on my right, continuing into the kitchen, as I search for him. "Where are you, Thad?" I call out. "I'm sorry dinner is late," I apologize. I look around my small eat-in kitchen. I have white appliances, countertops and cabinets with silver handles and a stainless steel sink with a window looking out into the backyard right above it. At one end, I have a door leading to a large pantry closet, while on the other end I have a small, rectangular, light pine kitchen table with four chairs and a sliding glass door leading out into the back. I step over to the table and hang my purse over the back of one of the chairs.

I walk back into the kitchen area, glancing at the few Christmas decorations I have in here. There's a snowman on one end of the counter and a Santa on the other. I have red and white Christmas kitchen towels and holiday liquid soap. I grab my cat's dinner bowl and a can of wet food. I flip the tab and pull, opening the food. Then I reach for a spoon and scoop all the food into his dish. I finally hear him as he comes scampering into the room, just as I finish. "Meow," he utters, as he looks up at me, asking for his meal.

"There you are," I croon, the moment I see him. "I'm so sorry!" I tap the spoon on the side of the dish and set it in the sink before I crouch down by Thaddeus. I set his food on the floor in front of him and announce, "Here you go." He's a precious, black and white tabby cat and I love being able to come home to him every night. I adoringly pat his head, while he immediately digs in to his dinner, bringing a smile to my face.

I stand up and turn back towards the counter. I grab the empty can of food and rinse it out before tossing it into my recycle container. Then I stand in front of my sink and wash my hands, as I look out the window into the dark night, but I only catch a faded glimpse of my reflection instead. I dry my hands and spin around, facing the refrigerator. I open it and peak inside, pulling out a strawberry yogurt. I close the door with my hip, as I pull off the top of the yogurt and then toss it in the garbage can under the sink. I grab a spoon out of the drawer next to the sink and wander over to the kitchen table. I pull out the chair by the back door and sit down before I dip my spoon into my yogurt and take a bite.

I heave a sigh and reach for my purse, knowing I don't want to wait too long to call about this job. I unzip my purse and reach into the side pocket. I pull out the piece of paper with the phone number for the referral Felicia gave me. I set the paper down on the table in front of me, before I zip my purse closed and loop it back over the chair next to me. Then, I take another bite of yogurt, before I pull out my cell phone and tap in the phone

37

number. I press the green button to connect the call and hold it to my ear. The woman answers almost immediately. "Hello?" Beth prompts.

I quickly swallow the yogurt in my mouth and set the spoon down on the table. "Hi, is this Beth Reynolds?" I inquire.

"Yes, it is," she confirms. "Who is this speaking, please?" she requests, a friendly tone in her voice.

"My name is Meredith Block," I inform her. "I own Merry Events in South Bristol. Felicia Johnson referred me," I add.

"Great!" she exclaims, startling me. "I'm so happy to speak with you," she claims, with an overabundance of cheerfulness.

"You are?" I prod. I have to admit, I'm a little surprised by her excitement.

"Of course! You're an event planner, right?" she verifies.

"Yes, I sure am," I proclaim. I'm incredibly proud of my new business. "What can I help you with?" I question.

"It's for my boss, actually," she corrects. "Chris Ackerman."

"I don't recognize the name," I murmur.

"I didn't think you would," she concedes. "He just inherited a house in Christmas Cove. His grandfather passed," she apprises me.

"Oh, I'm so sorry to hear that," I mumble, genuinely. "Right around the holidays too," I add. My heart clenches, as a rush of sadness washes over me for a man I don't even know. It has to be hard, especially this time of year.

"Yeah, it's really sad," she agrees, gently. "He was very close with his grandfather," she reveals.

"I can imagine, inheriting his house," I acknowledge, nodding my head, even though she can't see me. "But, how can I help you?" I prompt.

"There's a stipulation to the inheritance," she begins.

"Oh?" I prod.

"Yes. He must host Christmas for his family. Decorations, food and everything," she informs me. She sighs heavily and her tone changes slightly, sounding more casual. "I'm going to be honest here, I love my boss, but he doesn't know the first thing about entertaining," she admits.

I laugh, amused by her blunt comment. "Well, you're speaking with the right person," I announce.

"I certainly hope so," she grumbles. "It's a lot of work, but it pays well," she asserts.

"How many people will be there?" I inquire.

"Ten adults, a couple of them are teenagers," she advises.

"That's not so bad," I murmur.

"You'll have to decorate the entire home from top to bottom, interior and exterior," she elaborates.

My eyes widen in shock and I ask, "In one day?"

"No, of course not. Mr. Ackerman arrives tonight and hopes to hire someone by the weekend," she notifies me.

"Okay, that's plenty of time," I acknowledge. If I get the job, I would have a little less than two weeks before Christmas. I know I haven't seen the house yet, but it sounds like it's something I might be able to do by myself.

"They will need the entire Christmas dinner catered by a private chef on Christmas Day," she adds, suddenly sounding as if she's holding her breath.

"I take care of the cooking myself. What about Christmas Eve?" I question.

Her voice sounds a little tight as she answers, piquing my curiosity as to why she sounds so nervous. Is he difficult to work with or something? "There are no plans for Christmas Eve, so you can even take the night off. But you must work Christmas. That's non-negotiable," she emphasizes.

"Okay," I acknowledge. "Anything else?"

"Anything else?" she repeats, sounding shocked. "All the other people that I've spoken with have all but hung up on me when I told them that they have to work Christmas. Do you celebrate Christmas? I mean, are you familiar with the holiday?" she prompts, anxiously.

I laugh, finally understanding her nervous edge a moment ago. Then I reply, "Of course I'm familiar with Christmas. I'm familiar with all holidays. And I actually do celebrate Christmas, but my parents live in Baltimore, so I spend the holidays with friends," I enlighten her. "I'm sure they'll understand," I add.

She breathes a sigh of relief. Then she gleefully declares, "That's wonderful news."

"So, I have the job?" I prompt, excitement building up inside me.

"I wish I could hire you on the spot, but Mr. Ackerman wants to meet all of the applicants at the lake house tomorrow," she advises.

"Oh, I thought you said I was the only one left," I probe. I bite my bottom lip as disappointment washes over me.

"You are," she confirms, bringing a smile back to my face. "Can you be there at ten tomorrow morning?" she asks.

"Absolutely!" I agree. "What's the address?"

"I'll text it to you. Does this number work?" she questions.

"Sure does," I verify.

"Great. Thank you for your time," she acknowledges.

"Thank you," I reply, appreciatively. "Have a good night," I proclaim.

"You too!" Beth responds, before she disconnects the call.

I smile to myself as I glance at my phone, already deep in thought of how to approach my interview tomorrow morning. I set my phone down and release a sigh of satisfaction. Then I pick up my yogurt and my spoon and lean back in my chair. I scoop some yogurt onto my spoon and lift it to my mouth, taking a bite. I should get up early, so I have time to stop at the coffee shop before I drive over there.

My phone beeps, alerting me of a text. I reach over and grab my phone off the table, opening the text from Beth. "That was fast," I murmur to myself. I glance at the address and smile. "I know where that is," I mumble.

I text a quick reply, "Thank you."

"Well, Thaddeus, it looks like I have an interview tomorrow morning," I broadcast. He tilts his head, giving me a questioning look before he turns and runs into the living room, pouncing on something I can't see the moment he gets there, making me chuckle.

I finish my yogurt as I think about different ideas I could propose to Mr. Ackerman. I stand up and drop my spoon in the sink and toss the yogurt cup in the garbage. Then I make my way upstairs to get ready for bed and figure out what I'm going to wear tomorrow for my interview. I definitely want to make a good impression, even if I am the only one who shows up. This could be my very first client and my first job. I'm so excited!

41

I open my phone and scroll to my best friend's name. I find Bella and tap on the message icon. "Guess what?!?" She instantly responds with nothing but a question mark, before I can continue, making me laugh. "I have an interview at ten tomorrow with a Christmas client," I announce, without preamble.

"Sounds like the meeting went great tonight!" she replies. "Congratulations!" she exclaims, adding a confetti emoji.

"Thank you. I'll let you know how it goes. I have to go prepare," I add.

"Good luck!" she responds. "Let me know if you need help with anything," she offers.

I smile happily as I step into my bedroom and set my phone down on my dresser. I walk over to my closet and begin looking through my clothes and trying to decide what to wear for my interview tomorrow. I'm getting this job, I tell myself, boosting my self-confidence.

Chapter 5

Chris

I drive around the circle of the driveway and pull up next to the side of the garage. I put my SUV in park and push the button to turn it off. I slip my keys into my pocket and breathe another sigh of relief now that I'm here. I grab my black, leather briefcase off the passenger seat and step out of my car onto the gravel driveway and shut the door behind me. I look around into the familiar darkness, grateful the motion lights by the garage kicked in as I parked my car. You can't see anything without lights around here, like you can in the city. I sling my briefcase over my shoulder and stride around to the back of my car. I lift the tailgate and reach for my dark blue suitcase and pull it out of my truck. I set it down next to me, before I grab my black suitcase and pull it out of the back. My cell phone rings and I set my suitcase down next to the other one I already took out. Then, I reach into my pocket and pull out my phone. I glance at the screen and see Beth's face light it up. I immediately tap answer and put my phone to my ear, hoping she has good news for me. "Hi, Beth," I announce, hearing the exhaustion in my own voice.

"Hi, Mr. Ackerman," she replies. "Did you arrive yet?" she inquires.

"Yeah, I just pulled in," I concede, with a heavy sigh.

"Okay, great," she acknowledges. "Then I'll just give you what you need to know, so you can get settled and then we can finish up with the rest tomorrow," she politely offers.

"Thank you," I murmur, appreciatively.

"I contacted all the event planners in the area and it seems there's only one that's available for this job," she reveals. I wince in response. I hope the one that's available is good at their job. Usually, if someone is the only one left, there's cause to worry. Then again, at least there is one left. After all, it is the holiday season and everyone is busy this time of year. I would never be able to get everything done for Christmas and work full time without help. Honestly, it would be impossible. "The woman's name is Meredith Block from Merry Events," she continues. "I spoke with her earlier tonight and she does everything that you need," she enlightens me. "She'll be there to meet with you at ten tomorrow morning," she informs me.

"Thank you," I mumble, gratefully.

"I think that's it for tonight. We can discuss everything else when you get settled and organized," she advises.

"That's great Beth. Thanks," I reiterate. "I'll let you know how it goes with Ms. Block," I state. "Goodnight," I add.

"Goodnight, Mr. Ackerman," she replies.

I disconnect the call and slip my phone into my coat pocket. I grab my suitcases sitting next to me and walk past the two and a half car garage, listening to the sound of the gravel crunching under my feet. I step onto the paved walkway, making my way over to the front steps. I trudge up the five stone steps and set my bags down, with a heavy sigh. I bend down and reach for a small stone angel, sitting in the corner, right on the top landing. I pick it up and carefully flip it over, peaking underneath. I smile to myself at the sight of the familiar black key box with white lettering. I slide the door of the box open and slip the key out. "Right where he left it," I mumble to myself. I replace the lid on the key box and slip it into my coat pocket. No point in putting it away when there won't be a key inside. I bend down and return the stone angel to the corner of the porch.

Then, I step up to the front door, and take a deep breath, attempting to prepare myself for an onslaught of emotions. I pull the storm door open and stand in front of the thick, black, wooden door, with three, small, square windows cut out at the top, to let in a little bit of light. I tightly grasp the key and slip it into the lock. I turn the key until I hear the door click open. I right the key and pull it out of the lock. I slip the key in my pocket as I close my eyes, needing a moment to gather my strength to walk inside the house. I take a deep breath and exhale slowly one more time, hoping to calm my anxiety. I force myself to open my eyes. I stare at the door and softly murmur under my breath, "I can do this."

I grasp the handle and push the door open. I step into the dark house, the familiar scent of cedar, slamming into my chest and drowning me with memories. I blindly reach over to the wall with my hand, searching for the light switch and flip it on. The foyer suddenly floods with light and I blink a few times to adjust to the abrupt brightness. I attempt to gulp down the lump in my throat, as I turn around and reach for my suitcases, pulling them both inside, before closing the door behind me. I spin back around, the white, double-folding doors from the front closet on my right, with the stairs leading up to the bedrooms just beyond. The living room or great room is on my left and the kitchen and dining area straight ahead, with more beyond.

"Hi, Grandpa," I whisper reverently. I'm suddenly completely overwhelmed with my emotions. My chest aches and my gut twists into knots, as a painful, tingling sensation starts there and swiftly travels to the rest of my body. I miss him so much. It really hurts. Just being here is a lot to absorb. It almost feels like he's here with me, but I know he's not. I can't believe he's gone. I put my hand over my aching heart. I inhale deeply, before I take a hesitant step forward. I drop my suitcases and briefcase at the bottom of the stairs. Then I slip my coat off and drape it over the handle of my suitcase, leaving it all there for just a moment.

It feels surreal to be here without him, causing me to feel the need to look around and make sure everything is okay. I slowly take a step into the open dining room and kitchen area. It's the same area where we've spent many family meals together. Some have been for holidays or celebrations, while others have just been for simple visits at all different times of the year. My favorite times were almost always the summers, when we could really enjoy the lake. My eyes well up and spill over onto my cheeks. I'm no longer able to hold back my tears. I sniffle and allow them to fall freely, truly feeling the weight of not having him here for the first time. Every single spot of this house, both inside and out, holds so many special memories.

The dining room has heather gray walls with thick white moldings. A large, rectangular, lightly stained, oak dining table sits in the middle, with seating for ten people, although we've been known to squeeze more. To my right is a wide set of three stairs leading down to the game room, a full bath, a laundry room, a small family room and the garage followed by another set of stairs that leads to the basement, filled with a rec room, more bedrooms, another bathroom, my grandpa's workshop and some storage space. Just beyond the stairs is an ivory armoire loaded with vases, tablecloths and placemats, while on top, I find the familiar basket of silverware and napkins, along with a tray filled with both water glasses and wine glasses, dusty from lack of use. On the other side of the dining table is a set of sliding glass doors, leading out onto the back porch, overlooking the backyard, but it's too dark to see any of that tonight. To my left is a small oak cabinet with nothing but a blue runner and a white candle.

I wander past the cabinet and into the kitchen, the sound of my footsteps echoing on the wood floors. The kitchen has stainless steel appliances, ivory colored cabinets and tan granite countertop with flecks of gold, black and white. On the dining room side, five bar stools, with oak tops and black wrought iron wire legs, are pushed up under the overhang of the counter for additional seating. We definitely use every seat when the whole family is here.

I turn left, continuing my circle as I walk back into the living room. Several large windows cover the front of the room and a large white couch sits right underneath it, with an orange leather chair to the left of it, while directly across from it, sits an oversized, white loveseat. Covering the entire large wall in between is the white brick fireplace and white wooden mantle with built-in white bookshelves and cabinets on both sides.

I turn to my left where we usually place the big Christmas tree, but the space remains empty at the moment. I step up to the thermostat mounted on the wall. I adjust the temperature, hoping to warm up the house. Then I sniffle and brush my tears away. I take a deep breath and make my way back into the foyer.

I pick up my bags and carry them as I trudge up the stairs. I walk down the hallway, passing by scenic landscape pictures of Maine, that different family members have taken over the years as I make my way towards the bedrooms. The master bedroom and bathroom are located on this floor, along with two other spare bedrooms and another full bath, but I turn right into the first doorway out of habit. I walk up an additional five steps into a large room, with sloped ceilings. It's the same room that I always shared with my cousin, Jack Jr. and later on my cousin, Clint as well.

I set my bags down and leave them unopened, feeling completely exhausted. I sniff and wipe my tears again, not able to stop the flow or the ache in my chest. I trudge over to one of the full size beds on the other side of the room and sit down on the mattress. I take my shoes off and set them next to the bed. Then I roll back and lie down, fully clothed. I put my hands behind my head and stare up at the ceiling, letting my emotions completely take over for the moment. It all feels like too much and I don't think I have any other choice, than to give in. I wipe my eyes, but it does no good and I return my hand back behind my head. I attempt to gulp down the lump in my throat, while I think about grandpa. I take a deep breath and exhale slowly, allowing my eyes to flutter closed. I can feel the tension in my body slowly ease out of me as I finally start to relax. Images go through my mind like I'm watching a movie about him. Images of things like boating or fishing with my grandpa, while we laugh and talk about nothing, Sunday mornings when he would read the newspaper and watch all of us play in the backyard and just spending time together at family dinners and holidays. Before I know it, my thoughts and memories roll over into dreams, as I fall into a deep sleep.

My cell phone rings, pulling me out of sleep. I sit up to look for my phone and my head smashes into the ceiling with a bang. I groan, "Ugh," and drop back onto the mattress, one hand going to my head. I blink rapidly, trying to force my eyes open, as light streams in through the attic bedroom windows. I heave a sigh, finally realizing where I am. I lean over, searching for my phone on the floor next to me. I finally grasp my phone and pick it up. My mom's face lights up the screen and I quickly connect the call before it goes to voicemail. "Hello?" I groan into the phone. I grimace, rubbing at the lump forming on my head.

"Chris?" she questions. "Is everything all right?" she prompts. She already sounds worried with just my greeting.

I heave another sigh as I look down at myself, still wearing the same clothes I arrived in last night. "Yeah," I mumble and run my hand through my hair. "Hi, Mom," I murmur. I can't help, but picture her sitting at her white desk in her office, with pictures of the lake in Maine, displayed on the wall behind her, along with pictures of dad and me sitting on her desk in front of her. I cover my mouth as I yawn. "What time is it?" I inquire, rubbing my hand down my face.

"It's nine-thirty," she apprises me. "Were you sleeping?" she asks, surprised.

"Nine-thirty?" I question, astonished. I never sleep this late. No wonder she's so shocked. "I gotta' go, Mom. I have a meeting at ten," I enlighten her.

"A meeting?" she probes, sounding puzzled. "Aren't you in Maine?"

I nod my head, even though she can't see me and confirm, "Yes. It's for..." I trail off in hesitation. "It's fine. Don't worry," I insist.

"Is it the attorney?" she prods, curiously. "I know he needs to meet with you about Christmas," she reminds me.

I sit up and request, "Text me his number and I'll give him a call. I really gotta' go, Mom. I love you."

"Love you too, Honey," she replies and hangs up the phone.

I drop my phone on the bed and stand up, careful of the ceiling this time. I stride over to my suitcases and crouch down next to them. I unzip the black one and flip it open. I pull out a fresh pair of underwear, tan jeans and a rust colored, fitted, cable-knit sweater. Then I grab my brown loafers and some things I need for the bathroom, before I quickly make my way down the stairs and into the bathroom at the end of the hall. I have to clean myself up before the event planner shows up at my doorstep. I need to make a good impression. She's my only hope.

I quickly shower and get ready before I make my way downstairs. My stomach growls, loudly as I stride into the kitchen, headed right for the refrigerator. I pull it open and peak inside, finding it nearly empty. I grimace and shut the door, before I pull the freezer door open, with the same result. I heave a heavy sigh and make my way over to the cabinets, hoping I can find something, or maybe I can at least find some coffee to help keep me awake. I open cabinet after cabinet with no luck. "Great," I groan, in frustration. I don't have any food or coffee. I should've known. Well, I guess I'll have to wait to take care of that until after this interview is over, I grimace.

Chapter 6

Meredith

I look in the full-length mirror bolted to the back of my bathroom door, assessing my reflection. I want to be sure I make a good first impression on Mr. Ackerman for my interview. I really want this job. I'm wearing black fitted pants, a dark teal green ribbed turtleneck sweater and my favorite short, black velvet boots, with a two-inch heel. I have my hair parted in the front on the left side, then twisted loosely and pulled back on both sides into a low ponytail and then looped through the middle to add an extra twist, with the back falling in smooth curls. I reach for my red lipstick and remove the black cap. Then, I lean in towards the mirror above the sink and carefully apply it to my full lips. I firmly press my lips together and then pull them apart with a pop. I put the top back on my lipstick and pocket it, wanting to bring it along with me. I take one last glance in the mirror and smile to myself, satisfied. I pick up my phone, sitting on a shelf opposite the sink and then I scoop my silver dangling leaf earrings up off the white bathroom countertop. I open the door and make my way downstairs, putting my earrings in as I go.

I set my phone down on the table by the stairs and stride into the kitchen. I walk over to the chair where I left my purse last night. I pick up my purse and open it, slipping my lipstick inside, before closing it back up. I make my way over to the end of the counter and bend down, picking the cat dish up off the floor. I open the drawer on the end and grab a spoon, before I reach for a small can of cat food and swiftly pop the lid. I throw away the top under the sink. Then I scoop the food into his bowl and crouch down, placing it on the floor. "Thaddeus, breakfast!" I call out to my cat. I rinse the spoon and set it in the sink, before I do the same with the empty can and toss it in my recycle container under the sink.

I march through the living room and amble over to the front closet. I open the door and pull my navy blue quilted coat off the hanger and then shut the door. I slip my coat on and button it up, realizing I left my keys and purse in the kitchen. I need to get my head straight before this interview. This job is important to me. I continue to focus on each task I complete, making sure I don't forget to do anything, before I drive away. I make my way back to the kitchen table and pick up my purse and car keys, slipping the keys into my coat pocket. I glance over at Thaddeus, now eating his food and smile down at him. "See you later, Thad," I mumble, offering him a small wave, even though his eyes never roam from his food.

I walk towards the front door, grabbing my phone off the table as I walk by and slip it into my coat pocket on the way out the door. I pull the front door shut behind me, stopping to make sure it's locked. Then, I immediately make my way to my car. I slip in behind the wheel and set my purse down in the passenger seat next to me. I immediately buckle my seatbelt, before I start the car. I back out of my driveway and turn towards town. As I pull out onto the road, I finally allow my mind to wander to any questions I may need to address during the interview, instead of focusing on one task to the next, while I drive.

Only a few minutes later, I pull up in front of the local coffee shop. It's situated in a small strip of four shops, with the front nearly all glass to see inside.

Luckily, there doesn't appear to be many people inside now, so I should be able to make this quick. Usually, this place is so busy, especially in the summer when the tourists nearly take over the whole state, going on vacation. Everyone who lives around here though, knows they have the best pastries here and really good coffee as well as other specialty drinks.

I put my car in park and turn it off, immediately pocketing my keys. My phone rings and I reach for it, smiling at the sight of my best friend lighting up the screen. I press the answer button and greet her cheerfully, "Hi, Bella!"

"Hi, Meredith," she replies. "I'm just calling to wish you good luck with your interview," she enlightens me.

"Aw, thanks. That's so sweet," I express. Bella has been my best friend since we were kids. Many times I spent more time at her house, than my own because both of my parents were always so busy working. She feels like more of a sister to me, but then again, I don't have one of my own. Bella is beautiful with her thick, shoulder length black hair, big, almond-shaped brown eyes and lightly tanned skin. She always has a bright smile on her face for everyone, especially me.

"You're welcome," she responds.

"I actually just pulled up to the coffee shop in town. His assistant said he was arriving late last night, so I'm thinking he might not have coffee or food there this morning. So, I'm hoping a cup of coffee and a few pastries might help," I inform her.

"Great thinking," she acknowledges. "Why don't you come by the studio when you're finished and you can tell me how it went?" she suggests.

"That sounds good. I think I'll do that," I answer. "Thanks," I add, appreciatively as I unbuckle my seatbelt.

"I'll see you soon then," she replies.

"Okay. Bye, Bella," I respond. I hit end to disconnect the call and slip my phone back into my coat pocket. I grab my purse and climb out of the car onto the blacktop. I step up onto the sidewalk and pull the glass front door open.

I walk inside, my heels clicking on the tan tile floors, as the door swings closed behind me. I stop and inhale deeply, as a smile lights up my face at the scent of coffee, cinnamon and sugar. Small, square, two person, tan tables, with a stainless steel edge stand with a heavy, iron black pedestal, filling the customer side of the room, shaped in an L, although, some of the tables are pushed together to make bigger tables. A half-wall separates the seating area from the line of customers, feigning privacy. The far wall is currently decorated in a mural like chalk drawing for the holidays, consisting of a beautiful winter scene, including an adorable blue snowman, that's pointing towards some of the specials with his stick hand.

I scan the display cases in the front, filled with pies, cakes, bars, cookies, cupcakes, brownies, cheesecakes, muffins, croissants, donuts, scones and even yogurt parfaits. Then I glance up at the extensive menu of coffees, teas, lattes, espressos, smoothies and other specialty drinks, along with all the flavors that can be added. I grimace, not having a clue what to do. I should probably just go with something simple, since I have no idea what he even likes.

I step up to the counter, ready to order. The barista, Casey smiles at me as I approach. He's wearing the familiar uniform of black pants and a black t-shirt picturing their to-go cup in white. Above the cup it states, "Slay a Dragon with a Straw." He's twenty-four years old with blue eyes, short red hair and a closely trimmed beard and mustache. He's about five feet eight inches with broad shoulders and a lean build. He's a nice guy and always has a friendly smile on his face when I walk in.

"Good morning, Merry," he greets me, politely. "The usual?" he inquires, arching his eyebrows.

I smile in return and nod my head in confirmation. "Yes, please," I articulate. "And a medium black coffee with cream and sugar on the side. I'll take half a dozen donuts, too," I add, as an afterthought. I was only going to get one or two, but at least this way he'll have a few options.

"Oh," he murmurs. "Have a coffee date?" he probes.

I shake my head, feeling my cheeks turn a light shade of pink. "Oh, no. Not at all," I insist. "An interview, actually," I inform him.

His eyes widen in surprise and he comments, "I've never heard of bringing coffee to an interview."

I shrug my shoulders and give him a crooked smile. "Well, from what his assistant told me, he arrived late last night and is staying in a house where people haven't been in a while," I explain. "I'm sure he'll appreciate the coffee and donuts."

He nods his head in understanding and smiles. "Good idea. That will make an impression, I'm sure," he praises.

My face heats from his compliment and I shrug again, trying to brush it off. I don't know why I have so much trouble accepting compliments. At the same time, I do appreciate it. "That's the plan," I proclaim, keeping my smile in place.

He turns to the cash register and finishes putting my order in. Then, he looks back at me and meets my gaze. "That will be nine-fifty," he announces, with a smile.

I reach into my purse and pull out my long, black wallet. I open it and pull out a ten-dollar bill, and hold it out to him. "Here you go," I murmur.

He takes the money and puts it in the register, while I close my wallet and slip it back into my purse. I look up and Casey has his hand out, holding something out for me. "Your change," he apprises me.

"Thanks," I murmur. I hold out my hand and take it from him, dropping it right in the glass tip jar on the counter.

"And thank you," he replies, with a smile. "I'll put the creams and sugars in a bag for you," he advises me.

"Great," I respond, politely. I grin and patiently wait for him to put my order together.

It doesn't take long before he's handing me the two coffees in the travel cups with lids and decorative silver and white boxes with snowflakes on them and one donut inside each box. "There's a variety of donuts in those for you," he proclaims.

"Thank you, Casey," I tell him, gratefully. I pick up the bag, filled with the little boxes of donuts and then the cardboard container to carry the coffee cups. Then I cautiously spin around and make my way to the front door. I push it open with my back and step outside. I walk to my car and set the coffees down, while I open the door. I set my purse and the bag of donuts in the passenger seat. Then I climb in behind the wheel, before I pick the coffee up. I rearrange everything, making room in my cup holders for the coffee to keep it from spilling. I definitely don't want anything to happen to any of this on the way over.

I shut my door and pull my seatbelt over my chest and click it into place. Then I start my car and look around, before I cautiously pull away from the curb and drive the last few minutes to my interview.

I enter Christmas Cove and slow down, not wanting to miss the street between all the trees. I pull into a long gravel driveway, ending in a circle in front of the house. It's a large gray house with accents of red brick on the front left side of the house. The blue-gray shutters and black roof, compliment it perfectly. All kinds of trees line the driveway, with several of them being various types of pine trees. That's not really a surprise considering we're in Maine. With most of the trees bare for the winter, I notice neighbors on both sides, but not too close. I see an SUV off to the right of the garage and just beyond, a sprawling green lawn, appearing as if it leads all the way down to the water. "Wow, that's a lot of property and on the water too," I mumble to myself.

I pull a little further up and park my car in front of what appears to be a two and a half car garage attached to the house. I turn my car off and unbuckle my seatbelt. I pause, taking in my immediate surroundings. I notice a small stone fountain in the middle of the circle, with a bluestone path leading up to it. On each side, there appears to be a garden that's probably very colorful in the springtime, but is currently cut back for the winter. Two large oak trees and three large pine trees are scattered around the garden, with a beautiful Japanese Maple Tree, draping over the right side of the garden.

I smile to myself as I open the door, thinking about how much fun this could be. I can't wait to see the inside. I step out of the car and then reach back in to grab my purse and sling it over my shoulder. I reach in one more time to pick up the bag of donuts and the two coffees. I realize mine is almost gone and smirk. "Of course," I mumble to myself. I tip the cup back and quickly finish it off, before I drop it back in the cup holder. It will be easier to have one less thing to carry anyway. I take a step back from my car and shut the door with my hip. I take a deep breath and step towards the front door, instantly finding my heels a little shaky on the gravel. I slow down, not wanting to get hurt or drop anything. I look up, smiling at the American flag blowing in the wind. It's hanging off a short flagpole from a post on the red brick front porch.

I hear a door open and instantly slam closed, followed by footsteps quickly approaching. I pause and brace myself in anticipation, ready to meet Mr. Ackerman. He rounds the corner fast, nearly running into me and my eyes widen, in surprise. I smile wide and greet him, "Good morning." My breath catches as I quickly take him in, realizing he's not exactly what I was expecting.

Chapter 7

Chris

I jog out to my truck and open the tailgate. I pull out a couple boxes and hold them in front of me, carrying them into the house through the front door. Then I walk to the back of the house and set them down on the wood floor in the game room, before I turn around and quickly make my way back outside. I jog down the front steps and round the corner of the garage, freezing instantly, as I nearly bump right into a woman approaching the front walkway.

"Good morning!" she greets me, with a bright smile.

"Hi," I murmur, momentarily stunned by her beauty. "Can I help you?" I offer, as the corners of my mouth curve upwards.

"Are you Chris Ackerman?" she inquires.

"Depends on who's asking," I tease.

"I'm Meredith Block, from Merry Events. I spoke with Beth last night and she told me to be here at ten," she informs me.

I nod my head in acknowledgement. I didn't realize it was already ten. "Right," I mumble. "I'm sorry," I apologize. "I accidentally slept in this morning," I apprise her. "There's no coffee in the house, so I'm a little slow today," I concede. Her professional attire could've given her away as well. I'm just not thinking straight quite yet.

"Oh, well, here you go," she stammers. The corners of her lips twitch upwards as she holds a cup of coffee out to me.

"What's this?" I ask. I reach for the cup, hoping it's exactly what I think it is.

"Coffee. Black," she confirms. My eyes widen in surprise. "There's cream and sugar in the bag," she adds.

"Really?" I question, grateful. My hand wraps around the paper to-go cup, my hand instantly heating at the touch.

She shrugs and offers me a shy smile, her soft brown eyes sparkling. "Yes, well, Beth told me that you got in late last night and I figured there wasn't any coffee in the house," she explains. "There's donuts, too," she adds holding up a paper bag for me to see. "The best in town," she claims.

My mouth drops slightly open at her incredibly kind gesture. Before she has a chance to change her mind about this job, I blurt out, "You're hired."

She looks a little startled at my announcement and prompts, "Excuse me?"

"You're hired," I repeat, with more confidence. "Someone that considerate is exactly the kind of person I'm looking for to handle Christmas for my family," I emphasize.

"Really?" she prods.

She looks up at me, her soft brown eyes wide with astonishment. Then again, this wasn't really much of an interview, but I don't care. I already know I don't want to let her slip away. "Yes," I confirm, nodding my head. "Come on in and we can work out the details," I advise, gesturing towards the front door behind me. I turn around and walk up the steps, with Meredith following close behind. I pull open the screen door for her and gesture for her to go in front of me.

60

She steps inside and I guide her to the kitchen counter. "Have a seat," I offer, gesturing towards one of the bar stools. She takes off her coat and sets it down on a stool next to her, before she takes a seat. I stand on the opposite side and open the paper bag. I reach inside and pull out the sugar and cream. I swiftly make my coffee, adding two creams and one sugar. Then I take a deep breath, the scent alone, helping to wake me up, before I return my focus to Meredith.

"Don't you want to interview me, before you hire me?" she prompts, obviously puzzled.

I shake my head and reply, "No. Beth spoke with you. She told me that you're the only decorator available," I acknowledge.

"Event planner," she corrects, automatically.

My eyebrows draw down in confusion and I clarify, "Excuse me?"

She immediately elaborates, "I'm an event planner. I plan the event, decorate and cater."

My eyes widen, overwhelmed just thinking about doing all of those things for my family. "All by yourself?" I prompt.

She shrugs, indicating there's more to it than that. "Well, if it's a big event, I hire people to work with me," she explains.

"What constitutes a big event?" I ask.

"Fifty people or more. Like a wedding," she enlightens me.

I shake my head and insist, "Definitely not fifty people. Or a wedding," I declare. I feel my face heat almost instantly in embarrassment. I huff a laugh, "Hah," attempting to brush it off.

"Beth told me ten adults and a couple kids. That's easy," she acknowledges.

"Great," I reply. "Does twelve work for you?"

61

"Twelve people instead of ten?" she asks for clarification. "Sure," she proclaims, as if it's no big deal.

I shake my head and elaborate, "No, twelve thousand dollars."

Her eyes widen in shock. "Twelve thousand dollars?" she repeats. "For what?"

"I budgeted twelve thousand dollars for the decora..." I trail off and immediately correct myself. "Excuse me, the event planner. Plus decorations, food and whatever else might be needed," I rationalize.

"That's a big budget," she claims.

"Is it?" I prod. I don't think I took the cost difference between here and New York into consideration when I made the budget, but I guess it is a lot, especially for only one person.

She nods in affirmation, "Yes. It's very generous," she emphasizes.

"Okay, then," I acknowledge, not changing my offer. "When can you start?" I ask.

"Today," she blurts out. "I mean if that works for you," she adds, sheepishly, her cheeks turning a light shade of pink.

I nod my head in agreement. "Sure. I'll have Beth call you to send our contract," I advise. "Oh," I murmur and pull my wallet out of my back pocket. I pull out my credit card and hold it out for her. "Here," I offer.

"What's this?" she probes.

"My credit card. You can put all of your supplies on it," I notify her.

"Okay, great," she agrees. "Thanks."

How about a tour of the house?" I propose.

She nods in agreement, "Sure, that's a good place to start."

I push back from the counter and Meredith stands, following my lead. "Obviously this is the kitchen and dining room," I announce, a small smirk on my face.

She grins and playfully replies, "Obviously."

"We can add an extra table or two for dinner. That's what grandpa used to do," I reveal. I feel a pang in my chest, as his name falls from my mouth, but that's going to happen a lot. I take a deep breath, hoping to calm my anxiety.

"Sounds good," she acknowledges.

I gesture towards a small living room off the dining room that leads into the game room. "That's the living room. I'd like the small tree in there," I tell her.

She arches her eyebrows in question and asks, "There's more than one tree?"

I nod my head in confirmation and mumble, "Yes."

"Okay. It sounds like you know what you want," she murmurs.

"I just remember how my grandfather used to do it," I reiterate.

Her eyes soften and with her voice full of empathy, she acknowledges, "I can see you really loved him."

I offer her a sad smile and emphasize, "That I do." I flinch at my own words and immediately correct, "I did." I heave a sigh and softly concede, "I still do."

"I'm really sorry for your loss, Mr. Ackerman," she offers, sincerely.

I pinch my lips together as I nod my head in agreement. I exhale slowly and softly acknowledge, "Yeah, me too." I momentarily look away and focus on my breathing, needing a moment to pull myself together.

"Listen, Mr. Ackerman," Meredith begins.

I turn around and face her again. "Please, call me Chris," I request, immediately interrupting her.

She nods in acceptance, "Okay. Chris," she restates. An unexpected chill runs down my spine at the sound of my name on her lips. I quickly shake it off as she continues. "If you give me pictures of how he used to decorate this house, I'll do my best to match it," she proposes.

My eyes widen, loving that idea. I guess that's why she's the professional. "Really?" I prompt, excited at the prospect.

"Yes," she confirms. "You can even tell me what he used to cook and I'll do my best to honor him," she enlightens me.

I smile down at her, thrilled with her suggestion. "That would be really, really special, Meredith," I emphasize. "Thank you," I rasp, slightly emotional.

"Merry," she states.

I nod in agreement, "Yes, merry too."

She grins wide, clearly amused and shakes her head, correcting me again. "No, Merry. My name. My friends call me Merry," she explains awkwardly, widening my own smile.

"Then Merry it is," I announce. "Come on, I'll show you the rest of the house," I offer, encouraging her along.

We step back into the foyer, where we began. "This is the foyer," I announce the obvious. "It's the main entrance to the house. Everyone comes and goes through here, except if it's snowing," I explain.

"What happens if it's snowing?" she questions.

"They enter through the game room, downstairs," I advise.

"There's a game room downstairs?" she repeats.

I nod my head in response and give her a crooked smile. "Yeah, it's my favorite room. I'll show it to you last."

"Sounds good," she replies.

"Follow me," I instruct. Then I turn and walk upstairs and down the hall. I stop at the double doors, just before we round the corner and pull them open. "Linen closet," I announce.

"With linens?" she asks, peaking over my shoulder.

"Yes," I confirm.

"Great," she answers.

I gesture towards the door at the end of the hall and tell her, "Full bathroom." I step through the doorway next to the closet and walk up the stairs to the attic room. "This is one of the guest rooms," I announce.

She takes in the sloped ceiling, the unmade bed and my suitcases still open on the floor. "I take it you slept here last night," she observes.

"Yeah," I concur. "My cousins Jack, Clint and I used to share it," I reveal.

"Where are the other bedrooms?" she questions.

"Basement and second floor," I enlighten her.

She looks up and offers me a crooked smile. Then, she mumbles, "Old habits are hard to break, I guess."

I chuckle softly under my breath. "You could say that. I got in really late last night and it was the first room I thought of sleeping in," I admit.

"Hey, no need to explain yourself to me," she claims.

I feel my face heat and I quickly try to redirect. "Let's go downstairs. I duck my head as I walk down the steps, suddenly remembering to warn Merry as well. I turn my head and advise, "Watch your head," just as her head connects with the ceiling. I wince, as if feeling her pain.

She pulls back with a gasp and mumbles, "Ow."

"Sorry," I murmur, regretfully.

"It's okay," she claims, pasting a smile on her face.

We make our way downstairs, walk through the foyer and back into the living room. "This is the big tree room," I inform her.

She smirks and jokes, "I take it the big tree goes here?" She steps into the interior corner that poses as a barrier to walk around as you go from room to room.

I chuckle softly and nod my head. "Exactly," I proclaim. "When I was a kid, this is where the adults would hang out, while we were in the basement."

"And now?" she inquires.

"Well, last year my cousins and I were still in the game room, while the older adults were in here," I acknowledge.

She giggles softly, giving me goosebumps, but I quickly shake them off. "That sounds about right," she comments, the corners of her lips curving up in amusement. "So you want this to be a little more elegant, then?" she verifies.

"Yeah, maybe. Something different than the rest of the house," I acknowledge. "We exchange Christmas gifts here. It's the first room you see when you walk in. It's really special," I reveal.

"I can tell," she murmurs, appreciatively.

"This is where we take the family photos too," I add.

"I'll make it extra special," she emphasizes.

"You don't have to worry about the bedrooms. Maybe a little something, like a wreath or some candles," I suggest. "That's what grandpa used to do," I repeat.

"Got it," she declares and gives a firm nod of her head.

I look her in the eyes and inquire, "Any questions about the rooms you've seen so far?"

She shakes her head in response, "No. I might have some in the future, though."

"I'll be working from home, so I'll be here," I advise.

"Great," she states, smiling wide.

I grin and clap my hands together, before I announce, "Now on to the game room." She smiles and follows me back through the dining room and down the steps. We stride through the small family room, passing by the basement stairs on the right, before we finish in the game room. "Welcome to the game room," I broadcast, upon entering.

"Cozy," she murmurs, looking around the room. "I like it."

"The garage," I say, gesturing to my right, the moment we enter. "That's another full bath and then the laundry room," I enlighten her, pointing to the door directly across from the entrance. There's a chocolate brown, leather sectional couch to my left with a matching leather chair in the corner and a large square black table where we all used to play games, while growing up. Bookshelves line the opposite wall, loaded with various books, board games, cards, a game console, pictures and decorative accessories, with a flat screen TV mounted on the wall right above the middle section of the shelves. A second leather recliner in a dark red sits off to the right, in front of the bookshelf.

"Some of my best family memories were made here," I murmur, reverently. "My Uncle Jack taught me how to play hearts on this table," I reveal.

"Are you any good?" she prompts, curiously.

I smirk and brag lightheartedly. "Good enough to win a family championship three years in a row."

"Impressive," she croons.

I chuckles softly, momentarily getting lost in her smile. Then I clear my throat and quickly continue. "This room has an endless supply of snacks during the holidays.

People get lost down here for hours," I admit. "We usually surface when it's time to eat."

"So you want it decorated, but not too fancy," she proclaims.

"Yeah, basically," I concur.

"Got it," she states and pauses thoughtfully. "Pictures from past holidays will definitely help," she reiterates.

"I'll get you the photos by Friday," I advise.

"Great," she mumbles, appreciatively.

I gesture towards the sliding glass door, along the back wall. "That's the door we use when it snows. It's easier than walking up the stairs to the front door. We leave shoes there, so we don't track anything into the house," I explain.

"Smart," she acknowledges. We take a step closer to the door and peer out back. It leads to the lower level of the deck and out into the backyard. I smile at the sight of the bench swing, still hanging from the large oak tree with thick ropes. Then I glance a little further past the green grass, noticing the gray dock down by the water and the sea grass still appearing relatively green and strong for this time of year. "Beautiful," she murmurs.

I gulp down the lump in my throat and force myself to pull my attention away from the backyard and focus on Merry. "Thanks," I mumble.

"What about a slipper station?" she inquires, changing the subject.

"A slipper station?" I repeat, puzzled.

"Yes. A bunch of slippers and fuzzy socks for people to change into when they come in from the snow and then they can bring them home with them as a gift," she describes.

"I like that idea," I admit, grinning.

"I'll write out proposals for each room," she begins.

I shake my head, disrupting her train of thought. "No need. I trust you," I declare.

Her eyebrows draw down in confusion. She stares at me and emphasizes, "You don't even know me."

I nod my head in understanding and elaborate. "I can tell you understand me and how important Christmas is to my family. Are you sure you're okay spending Christmas working for me?" I question. I don't want her to feel pressured to take this job, even though I have no idea what I'd do without her.

"No problem at all," she instantly declares.

"I can let you go early so you can get to your family's house," I offer, as an alternative.

She grimaces and informs me, "They live in Maryland."

I feel a pinch in my chest, knowing she's so far away from her family for the holidays. "A friend maybe?" I prod.

She shrugs, like it's no big deal. "Maybe," she grumbles, obviously uncomfortable. "We'll see how it goes," she suggests.

I nod in agreement, "Okay. I need to get some work done," I inform her. I'm going to set my office up down here, so I'd appreciate it if you wouldn't come into this room between the hours of eight AM and seven PM during the week," I request.

"No problem," she concurs. "What about outside?"

"Grandpa did something different every year, but each year had a theme. One year was nutcrackers, another snowmen, and reindeer, as well as candy canes," I pause, "the list goes on and on. I think one of my favorites was the year he made a gingerbread house and covered the snow with a few lost presents from Santa."

"Wow," she murmurs, slightly in awe. "Do you have a theme in mind?" she probes.

"No," I respond as I shake my head. "You have cart blanche."

She grins and bounces briefly on her toes. "I like that," she proclaims.

"Thanks for coming by, Merry," I tell her, appreciatively. I hold out my hand towards her and she slips her small hand into mine, giving it a firm shake, at the same time a shock of electricity shoots up my arm.

"And thank you for hiring me," she declares, happily. "I look forward to hearing from Beth. I'll get on my designs today," she adds.

I walk her towards the front of the house and out to her car, thanking her one more time before I watch her pull out of the driveway. "I've got this," I assert, feeling confident about this Christmas, for the first time. At least I believe I do, now that I have Meredith in my corner.

Chapter 8

Meredith

I walk in the front door of the Franz music studio, named after my best friend Bella's family. Bella loves music and she's extremely talented. She has everything decorated beautifully for the holidays. There's a beautiful pine wreath on the front door with red berries, pinecones and a mesh green ribbon. Natural green garland wrapped with colored lights hangs over the door both inside and out. On the red wall to my left when I walk in, I find a black and white advent calendar bordered with red and white candy cane stripes, with Santa marking the calendar. While on the right a Santa image sits on the wall between the front door and the large picture window. Christmas cards from friends, family and customers borders the window overlooking the parking lot. On the big wall to the right, a set of piano keys are painted on the red walls with Franz Music Studio written in black underneath and a bench pushed up against it for customers. A small Santa sign stating, "Believe" hangs on the white door of one of the music rooms. Between two of the music room doors, sits a table with a lime green tablecloth and a gift basket, a guitar and a decorative sled sitting on top. Just beyond that sits another small table with a three foot Christmas tree decorated with musical notes, miniature instruments, Santa and colorful lights, with two mini wooden Santa chairs, along with a couple presents under the tree. On the big wall to my left, an enlarged piece of sheet music covers the entirety of the wall. A small white washed, antique accent table sits in front of it on the right, decorated with a miniature stage performance of the Nutcracker, a wooden nutcracker, a little bigger than the miniature stage and a snow globe with a winter scene on the bottom. She has a keyboard placed just in front of the wall with a door on each end leading to the large music room that she uses for groups, which even includes a small stage.

I spot Bella at the front of the room, behind the white washed front desk, with signs advertising various Christmas gift packages for lessons and instruments. She's wearing black jeans, casual, short, black boots and a long sleeved dark green V-neck sweater that ties in a knot at her waist. She looks up and smiles at me as I approach. "Hi, Mer!"

"Hi, Bella. This place looks really good!" I compliment.

"Thank you," she smiles, appreciatively. "How'd it go?" she inquires, leaning towards me over the counter.

"Do you have time?" I inquire, gesturing to a tall stool, matching the wood of the front desk.

"Of course," she declares. I slip my coat off and set it down on one of the stools and lower myself onto the one directly across from her. "Well?" she prompts.

I nod my head as a small smile lights up my face. "It went great. I got the job," I announce.

"That's fantastic!" she expresses.

"And he offered me twelve thousand dollars to do everything from now through Christmas," I elaborate.

Bella's mouth drops slightly open and her eyes widen in shock. "Twelve thousand dollars?" she reiterates, sounding dumbfounded.

"Shh!" I exclaim, desperately trying to quiet her down as quickly as possible. "Do you want everyone to hear?"

"Where does he get that kind of money?" she questions.

"He's some retail bigwig in Manhattan," I explain, as if that answers her question. "He has a good paying job, I guess," I add.

"Yeah, you think?" she challenges, wide-eyed.

"He seems to really want to make his family happy for Christmas," I proclaim.

"But Christmas Cove, Mer?" she prods. I know exactly what she's going to say before the words even leave her mouth. "That's a rough drive in bad weather," she reminds me, as if I didn't already know.

"I'll watch the forecasts," I insist.

"If you ever get stuck there, just call me and I'll take care of Thaddeus," she offers. I'm sure she just wants me to feel like I don't have to drive if the weather is bad.

"I'm not getting stuck there," I claim.

She smirks and suggests, "You might want to get stuck there."

"Bella! It's strictly business," I insist, feeling my face instantly turn cherry red. "Besides," I grimace and shrug, "I don't even know if he's single."

"If he wasn't, don't you think he'd bring his girlfriend with him?" she solicits, making me think about it more than I already have.

"I don't know," I murmur.

She arches her eyebrows in challenge, as the corners of her lips curve up. "Is he cute?" she probes.

I smile and lean a little bit closer to her as I admit, "Very. But he's really polished."

"There's nothing wrong with a little polish," she claims. She grins playfully.

"Bella, it's just business," I repeat.

She purses her lips and waves off my comment. "Yeah, Yeah," she mutters. "You said that already. Why don't you introduce him to me then?" she prods.

"No way!" I instantly refuse.

"Ooh, so there is some interest," she smirks, triumphantly.

I shake my head in denial. I can't be interested in him. This job is too important. "Of course not," I deny. "I just don't want you getting me into any trouble," I claim. "Wait until after Christmas and I'll introduce you," I suggest. My stomach twists at the thought, but I quickly shove it down.

"Deal," she agrees. She narrows her eyes in curiosity. "So, are you going to take the job?" she inquires.

"I'm ninety percent sure that I am," I acknowledge.

"I thought this was what you wanted," she mumbles. Suddenly, a look of understanding passes over her face and she sighs. Bella reaches over the counter and grabs my hand, giving it a light squeeze. She looks into my eyes, her gaze full of empathy. "Don't do this to yourself," she pleads.

I straighten, feeling defensive. "Do what?" I demand.

She offers me a sad smile and insists, "You know what, Merry. Not everyone has a close relationship with their parents," she claims, making me wince. She really does know me better than anyone.

"I don't know what you're talking about," I reply, sounding tense.

"Meredith Block," she argues. "I have been your best friend since we were twelve years old. You have spent every holiday with me since then," she reiterates what we both already know.

"So?" I challenge, defensively.

"So it's okay that your parents don't celebrate the holidays. It's okay that you don't see them all the time," she emphasizes, attempting to comfort me.

"Or any time at all," I grumble, bitterly.

"See?" she prods. "I knew it was that. Look, call them, if it's going to make you feel better," she proposes.

I feel my heart rate speed up, slightly panicked at her suggestion. "For what?" I question.

"Make sure they don't have special plans for the holidays," she elaborates. "You never know, right?"

I heave a nervous sigh. "Right. I guess," I mumble, reluctantly.

"Let me ask you something," she begins. "If your parents aren't doing anything for the holidays, would you take the job?"

I nod my head and confirm, "Absolutely."

"Then call them and ask," she encourages. "I mean, he's sending over a contract soon, right?" she prompts. I nod my head in response. "I'd want to sign that and send it in right away," she murmurs.

"Why?" I ask, even though I already know she's right. "His assistant said I was the only one interested in the job."

"Hey, you never know who might turn up," she emphasizes.

"True," I mumble in agreement.

"Call them," she demands.

"What? Now?" I ask, wide-eyed.

She nods her head in affirmation. "Yes. Right now. Call them," she reiterates.

I sigh in resignation. "Okay. Fine," I grumble. I reach over and grab my phone out of my purse. I scroll to my dad's name, Karl Block and tap it to connect the call. I put the phone to my ear and wait anxiously. My heart pounds so hard, I can hear its beat and the flow of my blood in my ears. My dad is just over six feet tall with a lean, but strong build. He has soft blue eyes and thick gray hair, always perfectly styled.

"Dr. Karl Block," he answers, professionally.

"I don't know why you answer the phone like that when you know it's me, Dad," I grumble.

"Well, hello there, Meredith. How are you?" he inquires, politely.

"Doing well, thanks. How are you?" I reply, automatically.

"Just great. Is everything okay?" he prods, as if that's the only reason I'd call.

I grimace before I respond. "Yes, of course. Just calling to chat. How is mom?" I prompt.

"She's fine. Working a lot. She's doing a lot of overtime during the holidays, so other doctors can spend them with their families," he advises.

"That's nice of her," I comment. I take a deep breath, attempting to build up my courage to ask. "I'm glad you brought up the holidays, Dad," I begin.

"Oh?" he questions, before changing direction. "Did you have a nice Thanksgiving with the Franz's?"

I sigh and proclaim, "Yes, it was wonderful." I close my eyes and take another deep breath. Then I quietly admit, "I really missed you guys."

"That's so sweet of you," he murmurs.

My heart clenches, wanting him to say more. I force myself to keep going. "Do you have any plans for the holidays?" I finally blurt out and then bite my lip nervously in anticipation.

"Plans for what?" he clarifies.

I release my lip and sigh heavily into the phone. "I don't know, Dad. Maybe spend Christmas with someone special," I urge.

"Like who?" he probes, naively, making me flinch. "Your mother is probably working," he reiterates.

"Me, Dad. Me!" I emphasize. "You know, your only daughter? The one that lives in your old house in Maine? The one that hasn't seen you in three years?" I add, heavy on my sarcasm.

"I don't understand why you're getting so upset, Meredith," he claims. "You're always welcome to come visit us down here in Baltimore. Our door is always open to you," he offers.

My shoulders sag in defeat. "That's not the point, Dad. I've spent every holiday since I was twelve with the Franz family," I reiterate.

"Oh, remind me to send them a gift basket," he replies.

I throw my hand up in aggravation. "Dad, come on," I complain.

"What, Meredith?" he questions. "I don't know what you are trying to get from me, Honey. I thought you and Isabella were best friends."

"We are, Dad," I confirm.

"Do you want some money so you can go on a cruise with her?" he offers.

"No, Dad," I mumble in disappointment. I shake my head, even though he can't see me. "Bella doesn't want to go on a cruise for Christmas," I insist.

Bella instantly straightens, looking at me with wide eyes. She reaches for a piece of paper and a pen and quickly scratches out a picture of a boat on the water. She holds the picture up to me and mouths the word, "Cruise?" in question. I ignore her as he continues.

"Then what is it?" he prods. "You're twenty-nine years old. Things haven't changed. Your mother and I have very important work to do. We are saving lives," he emphasizes.

I grimace and correct him. "I'm twenty-eight, Dad." I pause, giving in. "I thought that it might be different this year," I mumble, wanting to give him an excuse. "I was offered a really terrific opportunity, but I have to work on Christmas and I wanted to make sure you didn't have any surprises planned," I elaborate.

"Honey, you know how I feel about surprises," he reminds me. "Take the job. It will be good for you," he asserts.

"Good for me?" I repeat, confused.

"Sure," he acknowledges. "A little hard work never hurt anyone," he states, making me wince. "And I'm sure you'll be making a nice paycheck if you're working over the holidays. You can save it for a rainy day."

"Thanks, Dad," I mumble. "I'll talk to you later."

"I'll tell your mother you called. Goodbye," he tells me and I quickly disconnect the call.

I lean over and focus on slipping my phone back in my purse. I confident Bella knows I'm upset, but I don't want to let my emotions get the best of me right now. I look up and meet her gaze. "Happy?" I challenge.

She offers me a sad smile. Then she inquires, "Are you taking the job?"

"Yes," I confirm, assertively.

"Then, yes. I'm happy," she declares. She looks up at me with a question in her eyes and asks hesitantly, "Did he offer us a cruise for Christmas?"

I shake my head and sigh. "I don't want to talk about it," I grumble.

I stand up and grab my coat, quickly pulling it on. Bella walks around the counter and wraps me up in a hug. I lift my arms and hug her back, my heart both heavy and full at the same time. I guess that's normal for me. I squeeze her tight before I release her, incredibly grateful to have her in my life. She lets go and takes a step back.

"Merry, don't let it get you down. You've got an amazing job for Christmas," she praises. "It's your favorite holiday!"

I force a smile and nod my head in agreement. "I know," I concede.

"And you're going to do a great job," she proclaims.

My smile turns more genuine, as her constant support shines through. "I know," I smirk.

"And then Mr. Megabucks is going to sweep your best friend off her feet and whisk her away to New York City to live happily ever after," she jokes.

"Bell, Stop," I request. "Let me sulk."

She chuckles softly and replies, "No. This is a sulk-free zone. You're going to go home, sign that contract and get started turning this lake house into a winter wonderland."

"What would I do without you?" I prompt, truly thankful for my best friend.

She grins and lightheartedly announces, "The world will never know. Now, go!"

I smile again and pick up my purse, draping it over my shoulder. I spin back towards her and call, "Bye, Bella. Thank you." I stride out the front door, allowing her to get back to work, as I attempt to push the phone call with my dad out of my mind. "I've got this," I mumble to myself.

Chapter 9

Chris

I grab a cloth and a cleaning agent, immediately spraying the kitchen counter. I begin wiping it down, wanting to get everything clean. Everything seems dusty, with lack of use, but I guess that makes sense. Sometimes, it just doesn't really feel like it's been more than a few days since he's been gone, even though I know better. The doorbell rings, interrupting me. I heave a sigh and toss the rag into the sink. Then, I spin around and rush to the front door.

"Coming," I call out. I pull it open and breathe a sigh of relief at the sight of a woman standing on the other side of the door with numerous bags of groceries. She's in her early twenties, holding several of the bags, with even more bags sitting at her feet. She has light brown hair pulled up in a high ponytail and she's wearing faded blue jeans, a black t-shirt with a graphic design on the front, sneakers and an olive green, navy and brown, plaid, wool-lined winter coat, that she's left hanging open.

"Hi," she greets me, forcing a smile. "I have the groceries you ordered," she notifies me, stating the obvious.

"Oh, great," I murmur. "You can put these away in the kitchen back there," I advise, pointing straight to the back of the house.

She grimaces as she glances past me and then returns her narrowed gaze to me, looking at me as if I've lost my mind. "Put them away?" she repeats.

I nod my head in response. "Yeah. The fridge and freezer are empty. Wherever you want to put them is fine," I instruct.

She huffs a humorless laugh and shakes her head in refusal. "We don't do that. I'll put them on the table for you, but we don't put groceries away for people," she insists.

My eyebrows draw down in displeasure, not wanting to add even one more thing to my list of things I need to do right now. I prod, "Why not?"

"I don't know, Dude," she replies, sounding exasperated. "I just drop the groceries off," she reiterates.

She bends down and attempts to pick up as many bags as she can, letting me know this conversation is over. I heave a sigh and take a step towards her figuring I should assist. "Here, let me help you," I offer. I pick up some of the bags sitting near her feet and then, I pull the storm door open again, allowing her to go inside ahead of me.

"Thanks," she grumbles.

I nod in acknowledgement, even though she's not looking at me. "You can just put everything on the table," I advise, as we near the dining room table.

"Sure," she agrees.

We both set all the grocery bags down on the table. I pull my wallet out of my back pocket and skip over a five-dollar bill before I pull out a twenty. It is the holidays and I should tip like it. "Here you go," I offer, holding the money out to her.

She extends her hand and takes the money from me. Her eyes instantly light up in appreciation. "Thanks!" she exclaims, suddenly smiling wide. "Happy holidays," she proclaims, suddenly chipper. She spins on her heels and strides back towards the front door.

"You too," I acknowledge. She walks out, pulling the front door closed behind her.

I make quick work of putting the groceries away and tossing any expired food in the trash at the same time. I'll have to remember to take the garbage out later. I grimace, not remembering the garbage schedule around here. I'll have to look into that.

The doorbell rings again, interrupting my thoughts. I stride for the front door and pull it open. An unfamiliar man about six feet tall, with perfectly styled gray hair and friendly, coffee brown eyes stands on the doorstep wearing classic, black Oxford shoes. He's dressed up with a light blue button-down shirt, dark blue tie with very thin white stripes, navy blue dress pants, that appear to be part of a suit, but it's hard to tell with his long, black, wool dress coat pulled over the top. "Oh, hi," I greet him, surprised.

He arches his eyebrows in question at my reaction. "You were expecting someone else?" he prods.

I shake my head in response, "No." I quickly explain, "I just had a grocery delivery. I thought she had forgotten a bag or something." I pause and then ask, "Can I help you?"

The man holds his hand out to me, offering me his business card. I take it from him and wait for him to continue, barely glancing at the card. "I'm Artie Stein. I was Joseph Pasquarella's attorney," he announces. "I'm handling the execution of his will," he elaborates.

"Oh!" I reply, immediately recognizing his name. "Please, come in," I insist. I take a step back and hold my hand out, gesturing for him to come inside.

He steps into the entryway and the storm door closes behind him. "I assume you are Christian Ackerman, the deceased's grandson?" he inquires.

I force a stiff smile and nod sadly. "I am," I confirm.

He holds out a dark green bottle of white wine to me and nods towards me in offering. I take it from him and smile gratefully. "Very nice to meet you," he proclaims. "Your grandfather was a great man," he praises.

I look him in the eye, attempting to read him. It appears he's speaking from his personal experience with my grandfather. I gulp down the sudden lump in my throat at the sincerity I see reflected in his eyes. "Thank you," I acknowledge. "He certainly was," I agree. I clear my throat and stand a little straighter. Then, I offer, "Would you like a drink?" I hold up the bottle of wine he just handed me.

"No, thanks," he answers, with a polite smile. "This is a quick visit. I just wanted to introduce myself to you," he justifies.

"Well, it's nice to meet you as well," I murmur.

He nods in acknowledgment, before he continues. "Did your mother make you aware of the stipulation of your inheritance?" he probes, jumping right to business.

"To host Christmas?" I ask for clarification. He nods his head in confirmation and I simply answer, "Yes."

He casually glances around the immediate area and observes, "It doesn't look like you've done anything to decorate yet."

I heave a sigh and shake my head in response. "No, I haven't. I got in late last night," I reveal. He nods his head in understanding and I continue my explanation. "I just hired someone this morning to help me out with that."

He grins and expresses, "Terrific. I will be popping in on Christmas, just to make sure that everything is as your grandfather wanted," he informs me.

"Why don't you join us?" I propose, spontaneously.

His eyes widen instantly, appearing slightly startled by my offer. "For Christmas?" he asks for verification.

"Yes, for Christmas," I reiterate, with a firm nod of my head.

"I'd love to, but I don't want to leave my family. We usually get Chinese food for Christmas," he enlightens me, with a small smile.

"Well, come see what a Pasquarella Christmas is all about. Bring your family," I encourage. "We have plenty of room."

"You don't mind?" he questions. He continues without waiting for my response. "It's my wife and daughter," he notifies me, making sure it wouldn't be too many people.

I shake my head and smile, letting him know it's no big deal. Plus, if he knew grandpa well, I would like to get to know him and his family. "Not at all," I proclaim.

"Well, Hanukkah comes early this year," he recognizes, thinking out loud. "And we've never been to a family Christmas before," he admits, as a slow smile spreads across his face. "It could be fun," he declares.

"Trust me, it is," I confirm, grinning confidently. "Please," I plead. "I insist," I add.

Artie extends his hand out towards me. I meet him halfway, clasping his hand in mine. He gives my hand a firm shake. "Thank you," he replies, smiling appreciatively. "The Stein family graciously accepts," he happily announces, before we both drop our hands to our sides.

"Great," I express and return his smile. "I'll have Merry reach out with the details," I proclaim. I'm not quite sure what the plans are for Christmas myself at this point.

His eyes widen and he instantly prompts, "Merry? Merry Block?"

I nod my head in confirmation and reply, "Yes. She's the one that's helping me with Christmas," I explain.

"Good," he murmurs, obviously pleased.

"You know her?" I prod.

He nods his head, grinning in approval and answers, "I do. She planned my daughter's Bat Mitzvah," he reveals. "She's a good egg and really good at what she does," he adds, giving me his honest opinion.

"Thank you. That's really great to know," I recognize. The moment I met her, I already felt like I could trust her with making Christmas special for my family and me, but hearing him sing her praise, definitely increases my confidence in her even more. "Thanks for stopping by, Artie," I mumble, appreciatively.

"Absolutely," he acknowledges, with a firm nod of his head. "I'll see you on Christmas," he declares. "I'll bring the papers then too," he informs me.

"Papers? What papers?" I question, puzzled.

The corners of his mouth twitch up in amusement. "So that you can assume the deed, of course," he reminds me.

"Oh, of course," I murmur. I nod my head in agreement.

"Have a good day, Christian," he proclaims, smiling broadly. Then he turns back towards the front door and pushes it open.

"You too," I reply. I grin and he returns the gesture, just before he steps out the front door. The storm door swings shut and I close the front door behind him.

I turn back to the kitchen, just as my cell phone rings. I pull my phone out of my back pocket with a sigh. Everything already feels non-stop and I haven't really started anything yet. I see Beth's name light up my screen and tense, hoping she has good news. I tap the green button to answer the call and put my phone to my ear. "Hi, Beth," I greet her.

"Hi, Mr. Ackerman. I wanted to let you know that I just received the contract back from Merry Events, signed and ready to go," she enlightens me.

"That's great," I acknowledge. I exhale slowly and feel my shoulders instantly sag in relief. "Will you send me her contact information and send her my cell phone, so she's able to reach me if she needs to?" I request.

"Okay," she murmurs.

"Also, would you please let her know, she can just start tomorrow morning," I instruct. "I'm still trying to get everything cleaned up and ready for her to get started, so tomorrow would be perfect."

"Of course," she concurs. "I also wanted to let you know, I just sent you an email with your updated schedule on everything I moved around for you. Your first meeting is tomorrow morning at 11am, so you should have plenty of time to prepare."

"That will work out just fine," I confirm. "I should be organized here by the end of the day today and ready to get to work. Plus, if Merry comes earlier, she'll already be deep in her own work, while I'm on my calls," I update her. "I'll double check my schedule after we hang up to make sure it looks good from my end," I reiterate.

"Thank you," she replies. "Do you have anything else for me?" she questions.

"Not right now, thanks," I respond. "Let me know if anything comes up," I add.

"Absolutely and please let me know what you need from me. I'll talk to you tomorrow, then," she states.

"Okay, bye, Beth," I respond and disconnect the call.

I walk to the kitchen, the corners of my mouth tugging upwards, as I think about Merry. I'm grateful Beth found her. It seems she's exactly what I need if I'm going to get all of this done in time for Christmas. Now I just need to focus on my work. I set my cell phone down on the counter and then I reach for the rag I left in the sink continuing to clean up.

Chapter 10

Meredith

I step up to the mirror one more time to check my reflection. I'm wearing dark blue jeans, with a cranberry chenille turtleneck sweater and sturdy brown boots with a wool lining. I want to look nice and professional, but I also need to wear clothes and shoes I'm going to be able to really work in, especially since I'll be walking in and out of the house with a lot of boxes of decorations. The last thing I need would be to slip and fall and ruin the job before it begins. I run my hand over the top of my hair, smoothing out a few frayed hairs. Then I reach down towards the ends and gently scrunch my hair in my hand, enhancing the curls. I release it and smile, satisfied with having it down today in loose curls. I grab my red lipstick and pull off the cap. I run it over my lips, before rubbing my lips together and letting go, making a pop sound. I replace the top and slip it in my pocket, as I stride downstairs.

I make my way to the front closet and open the door, the same navy blue winter coat I wear regularly and immediately slipping it on. I walk over to the table by the stairs and pick up my phone slipping it inside my purse, along with my lipstick. Then I grab my keys and sling my purse over my shoulder. I glance back towards the kitchen and call out, "Bye, Thaddeus." I don't see him anywhere. He's probably sleeping now that his stomach is full.

I walk out to my car and slip in behind the wheel. I buckle my seat belt, start the car and back out of my driveway, immediately turning towards the highway. I take a deep breath, attempting to calm my nerves. I've been able to push them out of my mind and stomach, since I got the job, but now I have to really focus on doing a good job for Mr. Ackerman. "I mean Chris," I mumble, correcting my thought aloud. Now that it's time to work, my anxiety instantly comes flooding back.

I am really excited about this job. I've planned a lot of parties before, but that was before I really started my business. Granted those are the referrals that will hopefully help get Merry Events going, but a lot of them were family and close friends too. I love being able to plan parties for people and if I want my business to really flourish, I have to do a phenomenal job for Mr. Ackerman. He has a lot of very specific ideas about what he wants too and I don't want to disappoint him. Hopefully the pictures he said he would give me will help.

I pull into the gravel driveway and slowly drive my car around the circle. I park in front of the garage, wanting to be close to the house, knowing I have a lot of things to unload from the trunk. I bite my lip apprehensively, as I glance up at the house. Then I take a deep breath and shake it off. I mumble to myself, "You can do this," giving my confidence a much needed boost. I unbuckle my seat belt and turn the car off. I push the door open and climb out, striding right for the front door. I bypass the doorbell and knock, needing to put a little of my nervous energy into something, even if it's something small.

I hear footsteps approaching and the front door opens, revealing Chris. He pushes the storm door open and smiles down at me, the simple gesture giving me goosebumps, but I try to ignore them. He's wearing casual, light tan pants and a gray, half-zip, ribbed sweatshirt. I paste a smile on my face and greet him cheerfully, "Good morning!"

"Morning," he replies. "You can just walk in, you know," he advises.

"Thanks, but I don't have a key," I remind him.

"I'll give you the spare before you leave today," he offers, turning my smile genuine.

"Thank you," I murmur. I really appreciate the little things that make my job easier.

"You're welcome," he murmurs. "Coffee?" he proposes.

I step inside, brushing past him, before I turn around to face him. Then, I shake my head and reply, "No, thank you. I can take care of it," I insist, as he closes the door behind him.

He nods his head in affirmation and acknowledges, "Okay. I'm going to head to the game room to get some work done then. If you want to walk out that way, you'll see the path that goes around the house, so you'll know where it is, if you need it," he recommends.

"Okay," I agree and immediately follow him to the game room.

He unlocks the sliding glass door for me and pulls it open as he gestures out the door. "Just down the steps and then around to your right," he advises.

"Thank you," I murmur in appreciation. I walk outside, easily following the pathway around to my car. I open the trunk and pull out a big box of Christmas decorations. I turn around and immediately stride back towards the house. I walk back inside with the box in my arms, finding Chris focused on his computer. I squat and set the box down just inside the next room, hoping I don't disturb him. Then I spin around and I make my way back out to my car, continuing to unload all the boxes, until both the trunk and back seat are empty.

Chris

I look up from my computer as Meredith quietly walks back in with another box. I can't help but feel a little guilty watching her carry all those boxes inside, while I sit on my computer. Then again, that is why I hired her. She's obviously capable, but she shouldn't have to be doing all the heavy lifting on her own. I open my mouth to offer my help anyway, when my cell phone rings, stopping me. I tap the answer button without looking at the screen to see who's calling. "This is Chris," I murmur, staring after Meredith.

"Chris!" my boss's voice booms through the phone. "It's Larry," he announces.

I turn away from the door and Meredith working. The sound of Larry's tense voice immediately forces my attention back to my own work. "Oh, hey, Larry," I mumble. "How's everything in the office?" I inquire.

"Terrible," he blurts out.

"Terrible?" I repeat, puzzled. I sit a little straighter, anxious for what he has to say. "I haven't even been gone a day," I emphasize, surprised. I thought I had everything covered. What could I have possibly missed?

"Did you see the email about the strollers being recalled?" he challenges.

"What?" I gasp, in shock. "No!" I argue, hoping he's exaggerating, or it's something that's an easy fix. "When did you send it?" I prompt. I pull my laptop over to my lap and quickly pull up my email, impatiently waiting for the connection.

"Five minutes ago," he announces. "I thought you said that working remotely wasn't going to affect your performance?" he probes, irritably.

"It won't. It's not," I maintain, as I scroll through my email looking for his message. "I just got it," I confirm. I quickly skim through the email, a feeling of dread building in the pit of my stomach the further I read.

"So?" prods.

"This is the stroller that we based our new moms marketing campaign on," I declare. My heartbeat begins to race as panic sets in.

"I know," he spits out.

"It's going to be released at midnight," I proclaim, a little louder, as realization sets in of the disastrous effects this could have on the company.

"I'm aware," he grumbles.

I take a deep breath, hoping to calm myself down. "Okay," I murmur. "I need to fix this," I announce, vehemently.

"Get on it, Chris," he demands, before immediately disconnecting the call, without saying another word.

I heave a heavy sigh as I toss my phone on the couch next to me. I stand up and run my hand through my hair in frustration. I begin to pace the floor and talk out different scenarios in attempt to figure out how to solve this problem. I glance at my silver watch on my left wrist and grimace. I don't have a lot of time. I sigh again and continue pacing back and forth. I swiftly formulate an emergency plan in my head that I can easily manage from here.

Meredith

I walk upstairs with another box in my hands and into the master bedroom. The room has a queen-sized bed with a whitewashed, paneled headboard and footboard. There's a matching nightstand on each side of the bed with a small blue lamp, accessorized with a white lampshade. A matching, long dresser is on the wall to my right, just after the door leading to the master bathroom. While a tall, five-drawer armoire sits in the corner to the left of the sliding glass door. I walk through the room towards the sliding glass door and pull it open. I look outside and smile as I notice it leads out onto a large balcony, overlooking the backyard, with a view all the way down to the water. I smile to myself, knowing this will be perfect for something really special. It's absolutely beautiful, even in the middle of winter. I step out onto the balcony and look around, checking for outlets and to see where I'll be able to attach lights and specific decorations.

I hear a rolling sound I can't quite place and turn back towards the door to see if I can find the source. My eyes widen the moment I realize the door is sliding closed. I quickly lunge for the door, but I'm too late. I pull on the handle, attempting to open it. I yank a little harder and grimace, realizing it's locked. I heave a sigh, knowing I'm going to have to yell for Chris to come help me and it's only my first day. I knock loudly on the glass door and call, "Chris?" I knock again, a little harder and repeat myself, hoping he'll hear me, "Chris?"

"Hello?" I hear him shout back, sounding confused.

I try again, knocking even louder. "Chris?" I call out.

"Hello? Merry?" he yells, sounding as if he's a little closer.

"Chris!" I scream through the door. I continue, knocking and calling his name, until I see him stride through the bedroom door. I instantly smile and breathe a sigh of relief at the sight of him approaching me from inside.

He pulls the door open, his eyes wide with worry. "Merry, what are you doing out here?" he questions.

"Hanging some lights," I admit and shrug sheepishly.

"You need to prop the door open," he enlightens me. "It slides closed and locks," he states the same thing I just learned first hand.

"So I noticed," I smirk.

I walk back inside and close the door behind me. "Are you okay?" he prods.

I force a smile, feeling silly for locking myself out. I swiftly nod my head in acknowledgement, barely able to look him in the eyes. "Yes, of course," I confirm. "I'm sorry to have bothered you. You looked really busy."

He huffs a humorless laugh and concedes, "Just a little crisis at work."

"Is it fixed?" I ask, hopeful.

He shakes his head and sighs heavily. "Not yet. Almost," he amends, sounding hopeful. "Just a few more calls to make," he declares.

"Listen, I was going to do a tasting for you tonight, but I got a little carried away up here," I admit. "What if I make a meal that I could potentially make for Christmas dinner?" I propose, looking up at him from underneath my long lashes.

A slow grin spreads across his face. "That sounds terrific," he murmurs. "You don't mind?" he questions.

I shake my head and return his smile. "No, not at all," I maintain.

"Will you join me?" he prompts.

My eyes widen in surprise and I verify, "For dinner?"

"Yes," he confirms, his blue eyes sparkling. Then he straightens and begins to backtrack, "I mean, if you'd like. Strictly business, of course," he emphasizes, causing my hopeful heart to plummet to the pit of my stomach, even though I keep reminding myself he's off limits. He's my client. "So I can provide feedback," he elaborates.

I nod my head in agreement and paste a smile on my face. "Of course," I concur.

"Great," he mumbles.

"I'll clean up here and let you know when it's ready," I advise, hoping he'll go back to work now. I suddenly need to keep my hands busy and my mind occupied.

"Perfect," he affirms. "Thank you," he adds, gratefully.

I begin picking up some lights as he walks out of the room. I listen as his footsteps retreat down the stairs, before I drop the lights in my hands with a heavy sigh. "Come on Meredith, you can do this," I reiterate my mantra. This man does something to me. I have to stay focused on the job and away from this handsome man, I remind myself, again.

Chapter 11

Chris

I finish typing another email and press send, before I close my laptop with a heavy sigh. I stretch my legs out in front of me and stretch my arms above my head, feeling the need to move. I drop my hands back down to my face and rub my eyes, tired from staring at the computer for so long. My cell phone rings and I glance at the screen, a small smile playing on my lips as my mom's face fills the screen. I tap answer and lean back in the leather chair, as I put the phone to my ear. "Hello, Mother dear," I croon.

"Hi, Chris. I just finished work and I was thinking about you," she informs me.

"I just finished work myself," I murmur.

"Not working too hard, I hope," she prods.

"Probably as hard as you, Mom," I acknowledge.

"Touché," she mumbles. "I heard that you invited Artie Stein and his family over for Christmas," she proclaims.

"Shoot, I forgot to tell Meredith," I grumble, as I run my hand through my hair.

"Meredith? Who is Meredith?" mom questions, with extreme interest.

"You'll meet her, Mom. She's helping me with Christmas," I apprise her.

She gasps. "Oh, don't you tell me that you hired an event planner," she scolds me, accusingly.

I flinch in response. "Mom," I murmur her name, pleading for her to understand.

"That wasn't Grandpa's intention, Christian," she emphasizes, boldly.

"What do you mean?" I probe.

"He wanted you to connect with family to take on the Pasquarella family tradition. Grandpa did all of the cooking and decorating himself, you know," she reminds me. "Even when grandma was alive," she reminds me.

"I know, Mom. I've heard the stories," I concede. "I thought it would be a nice tradition to decorate with someone else," I advise. I wince, but I just can't admit the truth.

She breathes a sigh of relief. "As long as you didn't hire her," she reiterates.

I flinch and ask, "What's the difference?"

"Christian, have you paid this girl anything?" she repeats, reproachfully.

"No!" I declare, defensively. "She's upstairs cooking dinner right now," I add. I know exactly how my mom will take that statement, but I'm desperate.

"So," she begins, suddenly sounding much happier, "a romantic interest?" she inquires.

"Mom, come on," I prompt, not wanting to outright lie to my mother. Then again, I've already discovered Meredith to be absolutely beautiful, smart, kind, dedicated and a hard worker, what single man wouldn't be interested in her?

"Will she be there for Christmas?" she pushes.

"Yes," I concur, "and she loves cooking and decorating," I elaborate.

"Why have I never heard about her before?" she questions.

Meredith's voice calls from the kitchen announcing, "Dinner's ready!"

I fight a laugh and smile at her perfect timing. "Gotta' go, Mom. Dinner is ready," I inform her. "Love you," I declare.

"Christian!" I hear her call my name. She's obviously not finished grilling me yet, but I am finished talking about it. I disconnect the call and toss my phone onto the coffee table next to my laptop. I walk up the steps towards the kitchen, just as my cell phone rings again. The corners of my mouth twitch up in amusement, knowing it's my mom wanting more details, but I'm not answering her call right now.

I inhale deeply as I step into the room and my mouth instantly waters. "It smells delicious," I murmur.

She smiles up at me, appearing a little shy. "I hope you like it," she proclaims. She gestures towards the end of the dining room table and states, "Have a seat."

I look down at the table and smile at the two dinner settings placed together, at the end of the table. She has dark green place mats and simple white dishes, along with silverware and a water glass. I return my gaze to hers and inquire, "Do you want wine?"

"Do you have wine?" she answers with a question.

I grin and reply, "I sure do. Is white okay?"

"Perfect, actually," she acknowledges, smiling. "I made chicken," she elaborates, as she grabs the plates off the table and strides towards the kitchen.

I nod in understanding, knowing they go perfect together. I walk to the wine cabinet against the small wall in the middle of the room, separating us from the foyer and living room. I pull the door open and reach inside, grabbing the bottle of wine Artie Stein brought earlier, along with a corkscrew. I pull it out and close the cabinet. Then I grab two wine glasses from off the top of the hutch behind the table and bring it all back to the table. "My attorney brought wine," I enlighten her.

"Attorney?" she prompts.

"My grandfather's attorney, actually," I correct. "Just making sure I'm hosting Christmas, as per grandpa's wishes."

"Oh, I see," she claims and nods in understanding.

"Which reminds me," I murmur, as I remove the foil from the top of the bottle, "I invited him and his family to come for Christmas dinner," I advise.

"How many people?" she asks.

"Three," I declare. "Two adults and a child," I pause as I insert the corkscrew into the cork. "You know them actually," I inform her, beginning to twist the cork.

She turns towards me and approaches with two plates of food. She sets one down in each spot as she arches her eyebrows in curiosity. "I do?" she prods.

I nod my head in confirmation. "Yes. Artie Stein. He said you planned his daughter's Bat Mitzvah," I reveal.

Her whole face lights up as she smiles, broadly. "The Steins! Of course! They're really terrific people," she proclaims, as she lowers herself into the seat on the side of the table.

"He pretty much said the same about you," I enlighten her. "He also said you're really good at your job."

Her smile grows and her cheeks turn red at the compliment, causing my heart to skip a beat. "That's great to know. It will be nice having him here," she admits.

I clear my throat and pour two glasses of wine, setting the first in front of Merry and the second in front of the seat at the end of the table for myself. Then I sit down at the end, right next to Merry and smile. "So, what are we eating?" I ask.

"I made rosemary chicken in a garlic butter sauce, roasted Brussel sprouts, mashed potatoes and a green salad with balsamic vinegar and olive oil," she recites.

"Looks delicious," I declare, fighting a grimace. It does look incredibly good, but chicken doesn't work for Christmas. I'm just not sure how to tell her. I don't want her to feel bad after she obviously worked so hard on this dinner. Plus, it's probably something I should have already told her, I admit to myself, as a wave of guilt washes over me.

"But," she begins, looking at me through narrowed eyes.

"I didn't say, but," I insist, with a shake of my head. I take a bite of my potatoes, keeping my eyes focused on the food.

"I can see it in your eyes," she claims. "You're disappointed in something," she states, pushing for an answer.

I laugh in response. I can't help it. Here I am trying to hide something from her to spare her feelings and she doesn't let it slide, reading me better than almost anyone. "Am I that transparent?" I question.

She blushes a beautiful shade of pink and shrugs her shoulders in response. "Maybe a little," she concedes.

I give her a crooked smile and shake my head in disbelief. She's pretty amazing. I finally sigh and relent, "Okay, no chicken."

Her eyes widen in surprise and she prompts, "No chicken?"

I grimace and shake my head in answer. "It's too basic, I think. Grandpa went over the top with his cooking," I explain.

"No mashed potatoes either then?" she probes.

I take another bite and moan in satisfaction. "No, these are good," I declare. "There are some picky eaters and I think anyone would like these," I acknowledge.

"What about the Brussel sprouts?" she prods.

I chuckle and reply, "Give me a minute. I barely swallowed the potatoes."

Her cheeks turn an even darker shade of pink this time. "Right. Sorry," she mumbles, quickly apologizing.

I take a bite of the Brussel sprouts, the vegetable nearly melting in my mouth. "Mm," I mumble around the food. I swallow and point my fork at the Brussel sprouts and demand, "Definitely make these."

"Yeah?" she prompts, smiling.

I nod my head in affirmation. "Definitely," I reiterate. "The salad is fine too," I add, shrugging my shoulders, like it doesn't matter either way.

"Not too basic?" she prods, arching her eyebrows in challenge.

I smirk and question, "Isn't salad always basic?"

She shakes her head as the corners of her mouth tug upwards in amusement at my response. "I'll give you some more options," she announces. "We have a while to decide," she reminds me.

I nod in acknowledgement. "I definitely want the Brussel sprouts, though," I add, as I pop another one into my mouth. I'm incredibly impressed with how good these taste.

She nods in agreement and declares, "Okay, you got it."

I take a bite of the chicken and chew. I look at her and point to it with my fork, until I finish chewing. "I know I said no chicken, but I still want you to know, this is absolutely delicious," I compliment her.

She grins and mumbles, "Thank you." Then she takes a bite of her own dinner. We continue to eat for a few minutes in comfortable silence, the clinking of our forks the only sound.

When we're both nearly finished eating, I take a sip of my wine as I take her in, recognizing her natural beauty. I take a deep breath and quickly push the thought out of my head. I have too much going on right now to even think about a relationship. Plus, I live in New York and she lives here. It would never work.

"If this works for you," she starts, "I'm happy to continue making dinner for you, while we attempt to come up with a menu," she proposes.

My eyes widen in surprise. "You don't mind?" I clarify.

"Not at all," she admits.

A slow grin spread across my face and I appreciatively mumble, "You're going to spoil me."

She giggles and the sound sends a shock right through me. I take a deep breath and exhale slowly, calming my anxiety. She stands up and starts clearing the dishes. She's already done so much, so I put my hand out to stop her, gently resting my hand on her arm. Her eyes widen at my touch and I quickly pull my hand back. Then I blurt out, "I'll do the dishes, Merry. You don't have to wait on me," I insist. "Go on home," I encourage.

She nods her head in agreement, but doesn't put them back on the table. "Okay. I'll just leave them in the sink. But don't you want dessert?" she prods.

My eyes widen in surprise and I reiterate, "You made dessert?"

Her cheeks turn pink, as she concedes, "Only a little something. I wanted to gauge your sweet tooth," she adds. Then she shrugs her shoulders like it's no big deal.

I laugh in response. "I like sweets," I concur, "in moderation."

"Okay, tell me what you think of this," she requests. I watch as she walks over to the refrigerator and opens it. She reaches in and comes back out with two small bowls of something that looks very chocolaty and maybe topped with a dollop of whipped cream. She closes the refrigerator with her hip and returns to the table. She sets one down in front of me and places the other in front of her seat, as she sits back down.

"What's this?" I inquire.

"Homemade chocolate pudding with vanilla whipped cream," she describes.

"It looks too pretty to eat," I proclaim.

"Well, if you don't want it," she teases, reaching for my dessert.

I smirk and hold tight to my dessert cup. "I didn't say that," I insist, pulling it a little closer to me and out of her reach.

She smiles and watches me closely as I scoop a small bite and eat it. I close my eyes momentarily and sigh at the flood of memories that flash through my mind at the first taste of her dessert. "You like?" she prompts, anxiously.

I force myself to open my eyes and meet her gaze. I open my mouth to respond, but I'm not able to get the words out. I tear my gaze away from hers and take another bite of the dessert instead. "Are you okay?" she prods, her voice full of concern.

My heart leaps up to my throat and I nod my head. I gulp down the lump in my throat and barely croak out, "Yeah. I'm okay."

"You don't have to be nice. If you don't like it, just spit it out," she demands, making my lips quirk upwards in amusement.

"No, I love it," I declare, my face instantly falling. "It's really good," I add softer. "It's just," I pause and swallow over the lump in my throat again.

"Chris, what's wrong?" she questions. She reaches towards me in concern, without touching me.

I take another calming breath before I explain the feelings rushing through me. "Every year, my grandfather would make chocolate cream pie for dessert. This reminds me of it, that's all," I confess, feeling vulnerable. I look up at her and force a sad smile, hoping to ease her worry. "It's almost exactly like the way he used to make it. It's just missing the crust," I elaborate. "He called it Aunt Minnie's Chocolate Cream Pie."

She gasps and her eyes widen in shock. "Aunt Minnie?" she repeats for clarification.

I nod my head in confirmation. "Yeah, but I didn't have an Aunt Minnie," I reveal.

She grins wide and announces, "I did. This is her recipe."

I drop the spoon back into the dish and look at her, completely dumbfounded. "You're joking," I mutter.

Her grin grows. "No, really," she claims. "My grandfather's sister was Aunt Minnie. She was a baker and this was her chocolate cream pie recipe. She won a Christmas bake-off with it one year and her recipe was published in the local newspaper," she elaborates.

I huff a laugh and concede, "I bet that's where my grandfather got the recipe."

"I would have made the pie, but I didn't have time to make a crust for it," she admits.

I reach out and take her hands in mine on instinct. "Please make this for Christmas, Merry," I request. "Please," I plead. "My family will be blown away. Make it as a pie, though," I add.

Her face turns a deep shade of red as she looks into my eyes. "Absolutely. I promise," she proclaims, sounding a little bit breathless. "I'll make two so everyone can have some," she offers.

"Thank you," I express, appreciatively. "You don't know what it means to me," I add, feeling another lump form in my throat.

She smiles at me, giving me a look I can't quite decipher. Then she quietly mumbles, "I have an idea."

I realize I'm still holding her hands and instantly let them go. I clear my throat and sit back in my chair. "It's getting late," I announce.

"I'm sorry," she instantly apologizes. "I didn't mean to overstay my welcome."

My eyes widen and I shake my head in denial. "No, not at all. I appreciate dinner and dessert, especially dessert," I stress.

She giggles softly and murmurs, "I'm glad you enjoyed it."

"I don't want you to feel like you have to stay overtime, you know?" I prompt, hoping I'm not keeping her from anything, or anyone.

"No, I enjoy this. I really do," she claims, emphatically. "Plus, you're my only client this month. I want to make sure you're extra happy," she grins.

I return her smile and murmur my appreciation. "Thanks. I'll take it from here," I add, gesturing towards the dessert bowls.

"You sure?" she prods.

I nod my head in confirmation. "Yeah. Thanks." I suddenly remember I haven't given her a key yet. "Oh! Here," I blurt out. I pull a house key out of my pocket and hand it to her.

"The key to the house?" she clarifies.

I nod my head and mumble, "Yes."

"Great.   I'll get a key chain for it," she acknowledges.

"I'll walk you out," I offer. "Let me get my shoes."

She puts her hand up and shakes her head in refusal.   "No, it's okay.   I should leave right now. Thaddeus is probably annoyed that I haven't made dinner for him yet," she informs me.

My heart instantly sinks into the pit of my stomach at her words, causing my whole body to ache. She's with someone. I take a deep breath and force myself to speak. "Well, you don't want to keep him waiting," I reply, struggling to keep my emotions at bay.

"Have a good night, Chris," she proclaims and stands up. She grabs her coat off a chair at the other end of the table and slips it on, sending one more beautiful smile in my direction.

Goodnight," I rasp. I watch as she walks away, striding towards the front door. I take another deep breath and exhale slowly, as I softly remind myself, "You barely know her." I grimace, knowing I should keep my distance, no matter her circumstances, with so much going on right now. I guess I didn't expect to have such a strong reaction, when she said she had a boyfriend. I heave a sigh, in utter disappointment and take another bite of the dessert, savoring the flavor.

Chapter 12

Meredith

I walk into the flower shop in South Bristol, the floral scent nearly overwhelming me the moment I walk in. Garland wrapped with tiny white lights hangs throughout the store. It's added around the windows, the front counter, the doors, the shelves and even a few of the lights, both on the floor and hanging from the ceiling. Mistletoe hangs from the middle of a chandelier in the center of the shop. A large wreath decorated with fresh red and white poinsettia flowers hangs on the wall behind the register. I've never seen anything like it. The front of the shop is filled with all sizes of red and white poinsettias, amaryllis, cyclamen, a few Christmas Cacti, rosemary in the shape of mini Christmas trees, orchids, paperwhites and Christmas trees, all smaller than two feet tall. I smile to myself as I look around the quaint shop. Small gifts line the colorful wooden bookshelves including specialty vases, hand painted wineglasses, notes, wind chimes, decorative items for gardens, and floral accessories for around the house, including kitchen towels, figurines, candles, picture frames, floral landscape images and even books about flowers and gardening.

Daisy strolls in from the back room and smiles over at me. "Hi, Merry!" she greets me. She's about five feet five inches with dark brown hair, golden brown eyes and soft chocolate brown skin. We went to high school together and now we're both trying to get our feet off the ground with new local businesses, so we do what we can to support each other. She's dressed in dark blue jeans, a pale green long sleeved shirt with a dark green apron over the top and the name of her shop, "Daisy's," printed on the front of her apron in yellow and accented with a simple yellow and white daisy.

"Hi, Daisy," I reply cheerfully. "How's everything going?" I inquire.

"Pretty good with all the holiday orders," she informs me. "How about you? How's everything with Merry Events?" she questions.

"Great. I have a Christmas client in Christmas Cove that's going to keep me busy through the holiday," I enlighten her.

"Ah," she mumbles and nods her head in understanding. "So, I assume that's why you're here," she observes.

I nod my head in acknowledgement, "Yeah. I'd like to do something really special. It's kind of a big house and I want to make sure you see and smell Christmas everywhere," I explain. "Now I just have to figure out how to do that."

"Well, you could go with a combination if you'd like, or..." she trails off in thought. "What about poinsettias?" she suggests. "If the house is as big as you say, it's easy for me to get more of those for you," she informs me.

"Oh, I like that idea," I concur. I start to think about where I could put them around the house to add color. Plus, the whole house would smell amazing. "That sounds absolutely perfect," I agree. "Thank you," I add, sincerely.

"Of course," she murmurs. "Do you have any idea how many you'd like, or what sizes and colors?" she questions.

"Um," I mumble, uncertain.

She laughs in response. "Why don't you take a few of them today in a couple different sizes and then you can call me later with the full order," she proposes.

I exhale a sigh of relief. "Thank you. I think it will be much easier if I walk around the house and write it down as I go, instead of trying to do it from memory. I don't want to forget anything and not have the right sizes, or enough or have too many either," I add.

She walks towards a small spattering of plants and hands me two small ones before picking up a medium one herself. "We have small and medium ones in stock now, but I have even larger ones that have been coming in that are absolutely gorgeous," she apprises me.

"I think I'm going to want them in all three sizes. I just have to figure out exactly where for each," I concede. "I'll take a few of each of these right now and may I have an amaryllis and two mini Christmas trees as well?" I request. That should be enough to get me started.

"Of course," she agrees.

I follow her up to the cash register to pay. "Thank you for your help. You always have the best ideas with flowers," I insist.

"Thanks," she mumbles. "It's a good thing I own a flower shop, then," she jokes, making me giggle. She taps on the cash register and then announces, "$27.42." I pull out Chris's credit card and hand it to her. She reads the name on the card and looks up at me with an amused expression and a sparkle in her eyes. "So," she begins, as she runs the card through her machine. "Tell me all about this Christmas client you have," she requests, attempting to bring the focus back to me.

I can't stop the smile that lights up my face at the mention of Chris, but I try to stick to the facts. "Well, he just inherited his grandfather's home on the water there. He has to host a big family Christmas at the house. He's from New York, so he's working remotely from the house all month and I'm helping him with all the details for the celebration," I explain.

She nods her head in understanding, as she assesses me through narrowed eyes. She hands me a receipt to sign and I quickly scrawl my signature. "Is he cute?" she prods, innocently.

"Daisy!" I scold, feeling my face heat, almost instantly. I hand her back the signed receipt and slip the card back in my wallet.

She chuckles at my reaction and shrugs her shoulders, like it's no big deal. "What?" she prompts, arching her eyebrows in challenge.

"He's a client," I insist, meeting her gaze.

"So?" she probes. "You have single friends if you're not interested," she adds, when I make no effort to respond to her provocation.

I take a deep breath and shake my head in amusement, but ignore her comments. "Anyway," I emphasize, "I'm having a lot of fun with this job. Plus, I like keeping busy this time of year, so it works out perfectly."

She chuckles in response, but lets my change of subject slide. "Come on. I'll help you out to your car," she offers.

"Thanks," I mumble. I pick up the two small plants and spin on my heel, striding quickly for my car. I pop the trunk and we both set down the plants we're holding, before turning around to go back in and grab the rest of them I'm bringing to the house today. We walk back out to the car and she advises, "These are going to have to go on the floor in the back if you don't want anything to happen to them."

"You're right," I concur. We put the taller plants on the floor in the back of my car. Then, I close the back door followed by the trunk. I glance down at my cranberry V-neck sweater with white horizontal stripes and dark fitted jeans, dusting the dirt off of me. Then I look up at my friend and repeat, "Thanks, Daisy. I'll call you later today with the rest of the order. She nods her head and opens her mouth to say something, but I quickly interrupt. "Wait, can I just give you the card again over the phone?" I request.

"Yes, of course. No problem," she emphasizes. "I'll talk to you later, Merry."

"Thanks. Bye, Daisy!" I call. I walk around to the driver's seat of my car and slip in behind the wheel. She waves before she turns around and marches back into her shop.

I make my way to Chris's house, taking my time to keep the plants safe. Then I hop out and pop the trunk. I pull out the two smaller poinsettias and walk around the back to bring them inside. Chris is sitting on the couch, working on his laptop, wearing khaki pants and a navy blue, V-neck, pullover sweatshirt. I stomp the dirt off of my wool-lined, brown hiking boots, before I open the door and step inside. He looks up and smiles. "Hi, Meredith," he states, simply.

"Good morning. Do you mind if I put a few plants in here, so I can clean them up before I bring them around the house?" I request.

"Of course," he agrees. "Do you need help?" he asks, politely.

"No, thank you. I've got it," I proclaim.

I make three more trips out to my car to get all the flowers I brought home today. "That's it for now," I inform him. Then I go in search of a rag. I clean up the plants and then place them around the house. Leaving the Amaryllis on the wine cabinet in the kitchen and the mini Christmas tree on the hutch behind the dining room table. Then I pull my phone out to take notes and walk all the way upstairs. I want to start at the top and work my way down, counting how many of each size plant I would like for each room. Then, I'll call Daisy back with the full order.

After I finish my phone call with Daisy, I make my way into the foyer, with some thick green garland, white lights and red velvet bows. Then I grab a small ladder and begin hanging the garland, wrapping it with the white lights as I drape it around the large entryway closet. I add a bow in the middle and then another at each end, in the top corners, at the perfect angle. I stand back and realize I need something for the stairs. I find more garland, accented with miniature red and green presents. I take it and wrap it loosely around the banister, making sure there's still enough room to grab on to the railing, without the garland getting in the way. I stand back and take a look, assessing my work. I like it, but I may add more after I finish the rest of the house. I do still have the large poinsettias coming next week and I can put one in the corner between the stairs and the closet.

I glance at the time and gasp, realizing it's already after five. It feels like I just got here, but I have to get dinner started, if we want to eat at a reasonable time. I make my way to the kitchen and pull out the groceries I left in there earlier. I quickly get to work on the flank steak, roasted potatoes and honey and rosemary glazed carrots.

Just as I begin plating the food, Chris steps into the room. "It smells delicious in here," he mumbles, appreciatively.

"Thank you. Actually, I was just about to call you for dinner," I inform him. "Have a seat," I suggest.

"Thanks," he acknowledges and sits in the same chair at the end of the table. I finish filling the plates and walk over to the table, holding one in each hand. I set one down in front of him and the other in the seat next to him. "This looks delicious."

I smile in response. "If there's anything specific you would like, please let me know," I request. "Then, I can either make it for you to try my take on it, or we'll just add it to the menu."

"I do think we definitely need a turkey," he reveals.

He takes a bite of the potatoes and moans in appreciation, "Mm. These are delicious, but I think we should stick with the mashed potatoes you made last night for Christmas."

"Okay, sounds good," I acknowledge. "You know, I was thinking you might want a few things for the kids," I propose.

"That's a good idea," he admits. "I have a couple younger cousins," he declares.

"Maybe some homemade macaroni and cheese," I suggest.

"Sounds like something I'd like to eat," he grins at me, making me blush. "These carrots are delicious."

"I'll put all the things that you like on one list and we can narrow everything down closer to Christmas," I remind him.

He nods in acceptance and then takes a bite of the steak. He swallows his food and then he leans in towards me and inquires, "So what got you into event planning?"

"Well, I guess I just always love parties or celebrations of any kind, really," I admit. "When I was a little girl, I would plan these elaborate tea parties for all my stuffed animals," I confess, smiling at the memory.

He chuckles softly and murmurs, "I could see that."

He gives me a look that causes my heart to race and my face to suddenly feel like it's on fire. I can't believe that's how I shared my passion for planning parties with him. I didn't have to make it so personal. I have to remember this isn't a date. He's my client. This has to go well. Doing this could really help establish Merry Events and I can't mess that up. I need to go, before I say something I shouldn't. I take another bite and wipe my mouth on the napkin in my lap, before placing it back on the table. "I have to get home to feed Thaddeus," I reveal. He grimaces and nods his head in understanding, piquing my curiosity, but I don't ask any questions. Instead, I apprise him, "I'll be back by ten tomorrow."

"Okay. Thank you, Merry," he murmurs. "I'll take care of the dishes," he proclaims. I open my mouth to argue with him, but he immediately interrupts. "You cooked me a delicious meal, again," he emphasizes. "The least I can do is clean up," he insists.

I nod my head and smile in both appreciation and acknowledgement. "Thanks. I'll see you in the morning," I murmur. Then I push my chair back, scraping it against the wood floor and stand up.

"Bye, Meredith," he mumbles.

I grab my coat off the chair at the end of the table and slip it on. Then I sling my purse over my shoulder, wishing I didn't have to go, but knowing that's also the reason I have to. "Bye, Chris," I softly reply.

Chapter 13

Meredith

Over the next few days Chris and I fall into a routine. He works in the game room, while I decorate. I can't stop myself from sneaking glances at him, though, when I walk by, no matter how hard I try. Then we end every day eating dinner together, the conversations becoming more and more personal with every day that passes, but it's hard not to make it personal when you're really getting to know someone. Plus, I really enjoy spending time with him. Which makes it even harder to think about this job coming to an end and especially the thought of Chris going back to New York. I know he'll visit, since he does have a house here, but his job is there. He'll have to go back, eventually. I rub my chest, as a dull ache gnaws at me every time I think of him leaving, but I have no right to even think that way.

I assess my work, going over everything I've accomplished and what I'd still like to do. I hung small, wreaths on the doors of all the bedrooms and bathrooms. I added small accessories to those rooms as well, including Christmas hand towels and soap in the bathrooms. In the kitchen I added thick red ribbons with a large bow down the front of the cabinets, making them appear like wrapped gifts. I placed simple accessories around the tables as well as the counter, holiday signs on the walls, as well as several pictures from past Christmas celebrations, from the photos Chris gave to me and festive kitchen towels and candles. I even finished the basement and rec room. I just have to finish the big living room, where I'll put up the big Christmas tree and then the game room, as well as everything outside.

I grab another box of decorations and make my way to the living room, ready to continue decorating in there for the day. I set the box down and dust off my chenille, dark green turtleneck sweater and dark blue jeans out of habit. I push my long hair over my shoulder as I glance around the room, deciding where to start. Then I grab some garland and bows and make my way over to the fireplace. I string the garland, swinging it down in even swoops. I attach a red velvet bow right in the middle and then I set a two foot, bare, birch tree on each side of the fireplace. I sit down to attach a bow at the base of each tree.

Chris strides into the room wearing tan pants, a cranberry long-sleeved shirt with two buttons at the top and a charcoal cardigan over the top, hanging open. "Good morning," he greets me.

I spin in my seat towards him and look up and smile. "Good morning, Chris! I didn't disturb you, did I?" I prod.

He shakes his head and replies, "No, not at all."

"I'm almost done decorating up here. This is my last room and then I need to get into your office, or the game room," I tease, grinning.

He nods in acknowledgement. "Yeah, I figured as much."

"I can wait until the weekend, if that's better for you," I offer.

"Merry, you've been spending every single day here for nearly two weeks now. Don't you want a break?" he prompts.

I grimace and immediately apologize. "Oh, I'm sorry. Am I getting in the way?" I question, as a feeling of regret washes over me.

"No, not at all," he immediately insists. "I love having you around," he confesses, causing my cheeks to turn pink.

"You do?" I question, nervously.

"Well, yeah," he admits and attempts to shrug off his embarrassment. "The house is awfully quiet when you're not here," he concedes, his own cheeks turning a deep shade of red.

I smile, relief flooding me. "Well, that's what happens when you live alone. Part of the reason why I have Thaddeus," I reveal.

Chris winces and instantly looks away. He cautiously lowers himself down onto the edge of the loveseat. "Yeah, about Thaddeus," he mumbles, uncomfortably, "Do you want to invite him for Christmas?" he offers.

My eyebrows draw down in confusion. Invite him? "What?" I question, slightly perplexed.

"Well, you rush home every night, so he has dinner," he reiterates. He grimaces and then continues his explanation. "I kind of feel guilty that you've been having dinner here with me every night."

His clarification only leaves me feeling more confused. "Why?" I prompt.

He looks down at me and appears as if he forces out his next question. "Doesn't he mind that you're here?"

I hesitate, still puzzled, but give him an honest answer. "I'm sure he prefers me home, but that has no bearing on my work hours," I insist.

A look of determination passes over his face. "I'd be really upset if my girlfriend spent every waking hour with her boss, who just so happened to be a single guy," he blurts out.

My eyes widen, as my heart drops into my stomach at his admission. "Wait, your girlfriend?" I probe.

He shakes his head and reiterates, "No, not my girlfriend. I don't have a girlfriend."

"Chris, you're really confusing me. What does Thaddeus have to do with anything?" I ask, needing clarification.

He rubs his hands uncomfortably on his knees. "He's your boyfriend," he states, making me gasp. "Isn't he?" he pushes.

I burst out laughing. I can't help it. "My boyfriend?" I repeat, thoroughly amused.

"Yes. Don't you live with him?" he verifies.

I shake my head, not even trying to hide my amusement. "Of course I live with him. Chris," I prompt, making sure I have his full attention, "Thaddeus is my cat."

He gasps and repeats, "Your cat?"

I nod my head in response and laugh again. Chris quickly joins in, appearing relieved as he laughs along with me.

"I can't believe you thought Thaddeus was my boyfriend," I declare. "Wait until I tell Bella!" I mumble.

His face instantly turns a deep shade of red. "Oh, no," he grumbles. "Please don't tell anyone. Please," he pleads.

I grin and breathe my own sigh of relief. Then I reveal, "Chris, right now, you're all I've got for the holidays."

"Really?" he questions, surprised.

"Really," I repeat and nod in confirmation. "Before I took this job, I spoke with my dad about spending the holidays with me. He said that he and my mom are working all through the holidays and they just don't have time," I concede. My heart clenches tightly, but I take a deep breath and attempt to ignore it.

"I'm so sorry," he murmurs softly, his eyes full of empathy.

I shake my head as I gulp down the sudden lump in my throat. "No, it's fine," I mumble. "It's the same story every year. They're work-a-holics."

He offers me a sad smile and nods his head in understanding. "I get it. So am I," he admits.

"But you take time for family," I insist. "If you didn't, you wouldn't be here now." He nods in agreement and I continue, wanting to tell him more about me. "I'm their only child and I wasn't planned. They kind of just live their lives with me on the side."

He shakes his head and insists, "That can't be true."

I wince, "Unfortunately, it is. Then when I decided to start my own event planning business, forget it," I purse my lips in annoyance. "They don't even call me anymore. I went to an Ivy League school, just like they wanted, but I didn't follow in their footsteps."

"What do they do?" he inquires.

"Dad's a scientist and mom's a neurosurgeon," I answer.

"Oh, yeah," he mutters. "You're way," he emphasizes, dragging out the word, "on the opposite side of the spectrum."

I pinch my lips tightly together and nod my head in agreement. "And they remind me every chance they get," I concede.

"But you're really good at what you do, Merry," he praises me.

I huff a humorless laugh and exhale slowly. I feel myself relax, as I look into his eyes, seeing his sincerity in them. "Thank you. I appreciate that," I murmur. "But I hope you can understand why I'm throwing myself into my work," I add. "It's more than work for me. I get to plan the dream Christmas I always wanted," I confess.

Chris smiles brightly at me and my heart lurches in response. "I knew you were perfect," he mumbles.

My heart skips a beat and tingles spread throughout my body, heating me instantly. "Excuse me?" I prompt.

His cheeks turn pink and he quickly corrects himself. "For the job. Perfect for this job," he declares.

I nod in both understanding and disappointment. "Oh. Right," I mumble, pasting a fake smile on my face.

"I need to get back to work," he announces, suddenly. He quickly stands up and looks down at me, still sitting next to the fireplace. "Let me know when you want to start on the game room," he requests.

"Will do," I affirm.

I watch as he turns around and walks out of the room, heading towards the game room. I heave a sigh and turn back to the decorations, ready to lose myself in my work again. I finish the living room and glance at the time. "It's time to start dinner," I mumble to myself.

It's not long before I call Chris to the table, "Chris, dinner's ready."

He steps into the room and walks over to the wine cabinet. "Could I get you a glass of wine with dinner tonight?" he offers.

I smile and nod in appreciation. "I'd like that. Thank you."

"Red okay?" he adds, holding up a dark green bottle.

I nod in agreement, "That will be perfect with dinner."

I bring the plates over to the table, as he pours us both a glass of Cabernet Sauvignon. "Thank you," I murmur, as I sit down.

"Thank you," he repeats. He looks at me with an adoring grin on his face. I smile back at him, as my heart begins to pick up its pace. Something about this feels different. I'm not quite sure what it is, but I like it. He glances down at his plate and then returns his gaze to me. "So what's on the menu tonight?" he prompts.

I clear my throat and inform him, "We have filet mignon, with a béarnaise sauce if you'd like, roasted asparagus and a creamy shrimp risotto."

"Oh, wow," he murmurs, with awe. "You may have outdone yourself with this dish, Merry," he compliments.

"Well, try it first," I encourage.

I watch him as he takes a bite of the risotto and moans in appreciation. "Mm, delicious," he mumbles.

"Thanks," I reply and take a bite of the risotto.

He takes a bite of the filet and leans towards me, the corners of his mouth curving upwards. "So what do you like to do when you're not working yourself so hard, Meredith?" he inquires, his blue eyes full of curiosity.

My stomach twists into knots and I smile at him, wondering the same thing about him. I hear Bella's voice in my head, telling me I need to open up. I've already started to with Chris, especially earlier today. Maybe, it's time that I do a little bit more. I gulp, remembering that our time together is limited. Even though I know he'll be back, he lives and works in New York, I repeat in my head. "So?" he prompts, encouraging me. Well, maybe I should take advantage of the time we do have together and not worry so much about what happens when he leaves.

I look into his eyes, suddenly feeling at ease and I open my mouth to respond. "Well, I love spending time outdoors in the summer, especially on the lake," I add.

"This time of year, I guess I'm more simple. I like to spend time with people I care about and do things like cook and bake and plan parties for stuffed animals," I joke. He laughs and the soft sound as well as the light in his eyes, helps me to relax completely. "What about you?" I question.

"I like your list, except instead I'll eat whatever you make," he teases me back. We both laugh, the sound sending chills down my spine. I take another bite and listen to his gravelly voice reveal a little more about himself.

Chapter 14

Meredith

I open the glass door of Daisy's and step inside. I immediately spot her at the counter finishing up with a customer. I wave as she glances towards the doorway to see who walked in, before I turn to look around while I wait. I notice a beautiful new bouquet she put together, displayed in a large, red, square, Christmas tin, with an old wooden sleigh painted on the front. The festive bouquet includes red and white roses, pinecones, flat cedar, noble fir and white pine branches. I take a deep breath, inhaling the scent of roses and pine. I smile to myself, enjoying the display.

The man that was just at the counter walks by me and out the front door. I turn towards the back of the store and smile at Daisy, already approaching me. "Hi, Daisy," I greet her.

"Merry Christmas," she replies, a huge smile on her face. "How's everything going with the job?" she inquires.

"It's going great," I admit. I feel myself flush almost instantly, but I attempt to ignore it, hoping she will too.

She smirks, giving me a look full of curiosity, but to my relief, she doesn't push it. "I assume you're here to pick up your flower order," she recognizes.

I nod my head in confirmation, "Yes, I am."

"Do you want to meet me around back with your car and I'll help you load all the poinsettias into it?" she suggests. "It's a lot of flowers," she emphasizes.

"That sounds great," I acknowledge. "Thanks." She nods in acknowledgement. Then, she spins on her heel and steps towards the back, but I stop her before she gets too far. "Daisy," I call.

She spins back around to face me. "Yes," she prompts and arches her eyebrows in question.

"I would just like to add this to the order," I request. "This is absolutely perfect and it smells so good," I croon.

She chuckles in response and murmurs her agreement, "Yes, it does."

"Thank you," I reply. "I know just where I want to put it," I mumble to myself. It will look perfect on the coffee table in the big room and with the Christmas tree, that whole room won't only look like Christmas, it will also smell like it too.

"I'll just add it to your order and use the card you gave me for the file," she declares. "If that's okay with you?" she prods.

"That's great. Thanks," I mumble.

She nods her head in response. "Okay, good. I'll see you in a minute out back then," she proclaims. She turns around and walks into the back room of the flower shop, to I assume gather my order.

I pick up the red tin of flowers and gently cradle them in my right arm. Then, I spin on my heel and stride out the front door and back out to my car. I slip in behind the wheel and set the tin down on the floor in front of the passenger seat of the car. I start the car and swiftly drive around back, parking right in front of the back door. I want to make our trips back and forth with the flowers easier for both of us.

She swings the back door open, just as I step out of my car, the heavy door slamming into the bricks. She flinches and grumbles, "Oops," making me chuckle. "I'm stronger than I thought," she concedes and shrugs her shoulders, innocently. She looks at my car and back at me. "You know if you're going to be doing things like this a lot, you may want to invest in a bigger car, like an SUV or something," she suggests. "Plus, that would handle much better on our winter roads," she emphasizes.

"You saw my car yesterday. You knew what I had," I tease. She smirks and arches her eyebrows in challenge, making me roll my eyes in response. "I know, I know," I quickly placate her. "I will when I can, but this is what I've got for now," I answer honestly.

She nods her head in understanding and pauses, assessing my car. "Okay," she begins, "so, why don't we put the smaller ones in the trunk," she suggests. "All of them should be able to fit back there. Plus, they won't be damaged when you close the trunk, since you're not going far and they'll be able to come right out." She pauses and looks back at me with an arch of her eyebrows. "You are getting them right out, right?" she prompts.

"Yes, of course," I proclaim.

She nods in acceptance and continues. "Okay. The really big ones will probably be better on the floors. You can probably easily fit two on the floor in front, plus, two behind each seat. Then, you're going to have to put one in the seats and fill them in with the medium ones. They will hopefully stay up with the support of the other ones," she proposes.

"Okay, sounds good," I agree. I turn and pick up the smaller flowers and begin loading them into the trunk.

"If we can't get them all in without damaging them, I can always come by when Trey comes in for the afternoon shift," she informs me.

"Thanks Daisy," I murmur, truly grateful. She nods her head in acknowledgement. "Thank you for all of your help with these flowers," I reiterate. She always seems to know just what I need to make an event perfect. "I really appreciate it," I add.

She chuckles and replies, "It's my job, but you also know I'm always happy to help you out," she claims.

After the trunk is full, we start loading the back of the car, followed by the passenger side of the car. Soon my car is completely full of flowers. I glance around, but I don't see any more poinsettias. "Is that it?" I ask, hoping it is. There's not really room for anymore if I want to be able to drive.

She looks around and then opens the back door and peaks inside, before she turns back to me and nods her head in confirmation. "Yup, that's it," she declares. She carefully closes the passenger side door of my car, while I close the back door on the same side. "I can't believe we got all of them in there," she mumbles, as she shakes her head in disbelief. I laugh in response. "Drive really, really slow," she emphasizes, warning me.

I nod in acknowledgement and reply, "I will." I don't want anything to happen to any of these flowers either. "Thank you," I repeat.

"Let me know if you need anything else," she adds.

"Of course," I respond. I stride around to the driver's side of the car and slip in behind the wheel. "Goodbye," I call, just before I pull the door shut. I buckle my seat belt and start my car, before I turn and wave to Daisy. She waves back with a wide smile and turns to go back inside her shop, as I pull away.

I cautiously make my way to Chris's house, peering over the flowers with every single turn. I pull into the gravel driveway and come to a stop at the top of the circle by the garage. I put my car in park and breathe a heavy sigh of relief. I unbuckle my seat belt and turn the car off. I pop the trunk and step out of my car. Then I glance down at my outfit, making sure I'm not covered in dirt from carrying the flowers to the car. I'm wearing black leggings and black sneakers, with a fuzzy cranberry, mock turtleneck sweater, with my hair hanging down my back in loose curls. I don't see anything, but I swiftly dust myself off anyway, just to be sure. I walk around to the back of my car and I pick up the first two small poinsettias from the trunk and make my way around the house to the back door. I don't want to take a chance of tracking dirt through the house. That way, I can clean up what I need to on the plants, before I place them around the house.

I step inside and find Chris sitting on the couch, working on his laptop and dressed comfortably. He's wearing khaki pants, a dark, evergreen t-shirt, layered with a dark brown half-zip pullover on top. He looks up at me as I close the door behind me. "Hi, Chris," I greet him.

"Hi," he replies. He nods towards the plants in my hands and comments, "More poinsettias, I see."

I nod my head and murmur, "Yes." I hesitate momentarily before I request, "Actually, do you mind if I leave these in here, so I can clean them up before I put them around the house?" I pause and then quickly add, "I have more in my car." I don't want him to think these are the only two I'm referring to.

"No problem," he acknowledges. He offers me a sweet smile, before immediately going back to work.

I set the flowers down on the large rectangular coffee table and then step back outside, closing the door behind me. I make my way back around to my car, in front of the garage, grabbing more flowers. Then I continue making my way in and out of the house, with more and more flowers, saving the big ones to bring in last. Those are too heavy to carry more than one at a time. I walk in with the last poinsettia plant and set it down. I suddenly giggle as I take in the site of all the flowers in this room. Chris looks up from his work at the sound of my laughter. His head pops up from amongst a sea of red and I cover my mouth, trying to hide my amusement. He looks around the room, his eyes as wide as saucers. "Um," he mumbles, in surprise.

"I'm sorry," I apologize. "I'll get these out of here for you as quickly as possible," I proclaim. Then I immediately bite my lower lip in attempt to keep myself from laughing.

He bursts out laughing in response and I release the breath I didn't know I was holding, as I join him, laughing even harder. "That's a lot of flowers," he mumbles. He catches my eyes and grins playfully.

I shrug as if it's no big deal and contend, "Yeah, but they're going to look absolutely wonderful."

"I'm sure they will," he concurs.

I smile in response and feel my face heat almost instantly, happy with his small approval. I tear my gaze away from his and focus on the plants. "I should get these cleaned up," I murmur. I quickly stride towards the kitchen in search of a rag. I listen to the tapping of the keyboard, as I clean off all the plants. Then I make my way around the house with them one by one, finding the perfect spot to display each and every one.

After I finish the flowers I notice the dirt and fallen leaves on the table and floor of the game room. I'd like to clean up, but I don't want to bother him while he's working either. "I can vacuum and dust in here when you're taking a break. I don't want to leave you with this mess," I offer.

He looks up and quickly scans the room, before meeting my gaze. "Don't worry about it, Merry. I'll clean it up later," he insists.

"Thank you," I acknowledge, smiling appreciatively. He nods his head and turns back to his work.

I exit the room and make my way to the kitchen to start preparing dinner. There's a chill in the air today. A simple beef stew would be perfect for dinner on a day like this. I wash my hands and begin pulling out all the ingredients, immediately getting to work on our dinner. I gasp to myself, as the words 'our dinner' pass through my mind. I've started to think of it as our dinner, not dinner for a job, or even dinner for Chris; it's our dinner. I really enjoy having dinner with him every night. If I were home, I would be eating alone in my kitchen after feeding Thaddeus and probably checking my phone for messages, or scrolling through my emails and social media. But it's not even about being with someone else. It's about being with Chris. I really love spending time with him and getting to know him, as well as sharing things about me with him. I heave a heavy sigh. Maybe I'm letting myself get too involved with him by having dinner here every night. "He's a client," I remind myself out loud, again. But I'm not about to stop doing it either. I want everything to be perfect for him and his family for Christmas and the only way to really do that is to continue to put my whole heart and soul into this job, like I've been doing. I'm not about to hold myself back now because I'm starting to like him more than I should. "Oh, boy," I mumble to myself as I begin cutting up carrots.

I finish putting dinner in the crock-pot and make my way into the game room. I immediately notice Chris already cleaned up my mess. "Wow, it looks good in here," I compliment. He grins in response.

I glance out the sliding glass door and see a few snowflakes begin to fall. "Look, it's snowing," I murmur, a small smile on my face.

Chris looks outside and then back at me, before mumbling, "Beautiful."

I feel my face heat instantly, turning a deep red. I tear my gaze away from him and quickly look for something to do. I make my way to the corner and pull the five-foot artificial tree out of the box and begin putting it together. I should be able to set this up and have it decorated before dinner is ready. I might even have time to finish the room. I just have to keep my focus on work and not the man working on the couch right behind me.

Chapter 15

Meredith

Over the next few days I'm able to maintain my focus on my job and put my heart fully into my work. I really enjoy decorating Chris's house. His home is beautiful. Plus, I'm having fun working on all the little extras for the party, as well as the food and the menu, especially trying different things with Chris. Today, I've been spending the whole day baking all kinds of Christmas cookies. I have the kitchen and dining room covered with cooling racks and wax paper, so I'm able to cool and decorate all of the different colorful and delectable treats.

I walk up to my completed gingerbread train and gently check to make sure the frosting is dry. Satisfied, I carefully pick it up, piece by piece, and place it on a large, rectangular, winter white platter in the center of the kitchen counter, hoping to keep it safe. I just made an engine with Santa driving the train and two open cars trailing behind, with gingerbread elves riding inside each car. When I have the train exactly how I want it, I turn around and pick up the tray of gingerbread cookies that I baked with the remaining dough left over from creating the train. I take my time spreading the cookies out around the train on the outside of the platter. I don't want anything to happen to the train now that it's all done, but it should be fine away from the edge of the counter.

I hear the soft tap of approaching footsteps and look up just as Chris wanders into the kitchen. I smile as I watch his eyes widen while he looks around the room, taking in the enormous spread of cookies. I keep my eyes on him, wanting to see his reaction. He stops and closes his eyes, before he takes a deep breath. The corners of his mouth curve upwards, as he inhales the sweet scents of sugar, chocolate, cinnamon and so much more. He opens his eyes and looks at me, grinning broadly. "Wow," he mumbles, seeming a little in awe. "These look amazing and smell absolutely delicious," he praises me.

"Thank you," I mumble, with an appreciative smile on my face. "Go ahead, try one," I insist and nod in encouragement.

His face lights up, his blue eyes sparkling. His smile reminds me of a child's on Christmas morning, as he looks at all of the treats, trying to decide which one to try first. He eventually grabs a frosted cutout cookie shaped like a candy cane and a peanut butter blossom topped with a Hershey kiss. He glances at me and smirks unapologetically. Then he shrugs his shoulders, as if telling me he couldn't help himself. I can't help, but giggle in response, as I return my attention to baking the next batch of cookies.

The next few days, I begin to tackle the decorations and lights on the outside of the house. It's easier to keep my focus on my job, without Chris so close by. I want to turn the outside into a sort of winter wonderland and enhancing a theme in the back of the house, following his family traditions. I decorated most of the front first, keeping it simple with garland wrapped with white lights around the front door, the windows, the white poles and both sides of the two-car garage. I hung a beautiful wreath, decorated with red berries, pine cones and wrapped with a red velvet ribbon, tied at the top in an elaborate bow, centered above the two garages. Then I hung a matching smaller wreath on the front door. I decorated the pine trees along the driveway and in the middle of the circle, alternating white and blue lights. Then I twisted them together to highlight the small fountain in the middle of the circle and tie the white and blue theme together, since I'll be using mostly blue lights in the back. Today I'm ready to tackle the roof and the back of the house. I dressed warm, knowing I'm going to be spending most of the day outside, but I still wonder if I'll need another layer. I'm wearing a tan V-neck sweater and dark blue jeans, with my short, wool-lined, brown boots, along with my familiar navy blue quilted jacket.

I pull two large boxes, filled with lights out of my car and set them on the ground. I close my trunk and look around. I take a deep breath and exhale slowly, feeling a damp, chilliness in the air. It's the kind of chill that I can feel all the way to my bones. "It definitely feels like snow," I mumble to myself. The corners of my lips curve up in a smile. Snow would be wonderful. I would love to have a white Christmas this year. Snow has a way of adding to the decorations and festivities, without me having to do anything. I bend down and pick up the boxes, before I make my way around to the back deck. Then, I stride back around to the front of the house and into the garage. I walk inside and leaning up against the far wall, I find a tall silver ladder I can lean against the house to climb up to the roof. I lift it up off the hooks and carefully ease it out of the garage. I half carry and half drag the ladder around to the back of the house and climb to the upper deck, before I lean it against the house. I grip the sides of the ladder and wiggle it just a little bit trying to make sure it's sturdy. "I think it's good," I mumble to myself.

I walk over to the box of lights and pull out a new string of blue lights. Then I climb up the ladder and hold the lights up to the gutter, trying to decide exactly how I want to hang them along the roofline. "Hey," Chris calls. The sound of his voice startles me causing me to jump. I grasp the ladder tightly and attempt to maintain my balance. He steps outside and I quickly take him in. He's wearing his familiar khaki pants and an evergreen V-neck sweater, along with his brown loafers. He slides the door closed behind him, as he pulls his short charcoal gray, wool coat on over the top.

"Hey yourself," I grumble. I breathe a sigh of relief, struggling to slow my heartbeat back to its normal pace.

"What are you doing?" he asks, his tone worried.

"Setting up the lights on the roof," I answer, as if it should be obvious.

"Why?" he prompts.

I purse my lips and arch my eyebrows in question, slightly confused why he's asking. Then, I sarcastically remind him, "Because it's my job."

He winces in response. Then he clears his throat and refocuses on me. "That's really high Meredith," he claims.

"Don't be silly," I declare, attempting to wave off his concern. "I'm not afraid of heights," I proclaim.

"Why don't you just go out on the balcony?" he suggests.

I grimace and defiantly reply, "Because I don't want to leave the door open or track dirt into the house."

"Meredith, this is dangerous," he emphasizes.

"No, it's not," I insist, shaking my head. "I've strung lights on my roof every year since I was twelve years old and it's much higher than this," I reveal.

"Can I at least hand you the lights from inside?" he pleads.

I heave a sigh. "Fine," I grumble, relenting.

"And you can get onto the roof from the balcony, you know," he reminds me.

"Yeah, I guess," I agree.

"Or we could even clean up whatever snow and dirt you track in," he proposes. "I don't mind," he contends.

"I'm not leaving the door open," I announce, defiantly. "I don't want my decorations to blow down inside," I elaborate.

"You can just crack it open," he reiterates. "Come on," he encourages. He grabs both boxes off the ground as I step down from the ladder and reluctantly follow him inside.

I slip off my coat and put it over a chair in the kitchen, before I spin around and have to hurry to catch up with Chris. He strides upstairs and I chase after him. "Chris, Stop," I call out, as I catch up to him in the hallway.

He slowly turns around and faces me as his eyebrows draw down in confusion. "What?" he inquires.

"You are doing my job," I emphasize.

"But I want to help," he insists.

I grimace, but I understand where he's coming from. "I know," I murmur, "but it makes me feel bad," I proclaim.

Chris looks at me quizzically and finally nods in understanding. He heaves a sigh and relents. Then, he carefully hands me one box and sets the other one on the floor in the hallway. "Don't forget to prop the door open so you can get back in," he reminds me. "In case I'm not back yet," he adds, letting me know he's leaving.

"Where are you going?" I question.

"Oh, I have an appointment in town," he explains, gesturing over his shoulder. "I'll be an hour, maybe two," he advises.

"Okay," I murmur, nodding my head in acknowledgement. "Thank you."

For a moment, he doesn't move. He just stares at me, hesitant, before he finally nods his head in acceptance and forces himself to smile. Then he reluctantly turns to leave. I watch him walk down the stairs, before I spin back around and stride into the master bedroom. I set the box down in front of the sliding glass door and step back out into the hall to grab the other one I made Chris leave out there. I bring it into the room and set it down. Then I open the sliding glass door and prop it open with a small box, just as Chris instructed.

I begin wrapping blue lights around the rails of the balcony. I finish the strand of lights in my hand and turn to grab more from one of the boxes just inside the door. I squat down and pick up the box. Then I turn back towards the door and carry it out on the balcony with me, accidentally bumping the box on the floor propping the door open. I quickly set down the box I'm holding and lunge for the door, trying to stop it from closing. "Oh, no!" I gasp. The door suddenly clicks shut and my stomach twists into knots, already knowing I'm trapped. I reach the door and tug anyway, but nothing happens. I wince and yank harder, but it doesn't move. I exhale harshly as my shoulders sag in defeat. "Just great," I grumble, knowing Chris is gone and won't be back for a couple hours. I might as well get more of this done.

I peak inside the box I just brought outside and instantly realize I grabbed the wrong one. I groan in irritation as I glare down at it, knowing more than half the stuff I need is still inside. There's not really much I can do until I can get the rest of the lights. "Awesome," I mumble, sarcastically. "Now I'm stuck out here and I can't even get anything done." I heave a sigh in defeat and cross my arms over my chest, attempting to protect myself from the sudden damp chill in the air. I rub my arms, wishing I didn't just take off my coat, for more than one reason. Besides being cold, I left my phone in my coat pocket and I can't even call for help. I lean against the door and slowly slide down the glass, until I'm sitting on the wooden slats of the balcony. I pull my knees up to my chest and wrap my arms around them, attempting to keep myself warm. I look out at the back yard and the lake just beyond, as I put a mental list together of things I still need to accomplish, especially now that I'm losing time sitting out here and getting nothing done.

I rub my arms and legs again to warm them up and then I rest my head on my knees in defeat. I'm tired, cold and frustrated. I finally let my mind wander to Chris. The same man I thought I could push out of my thoughts by working outside and putting some space between us. "Well, I guess this is one way to do it," I murmur and laugh humorlessly at my situation. It's not working anyway. I can't stop thinking about him. I guess it makes sense when I'm spending so much time with him in his home, getting ready for Christmas with his family. This feels like so much more than a job. I don't know how this happened. Now I have to wait for him to come rescue me. I glance up at the sky, hoping he'll be here soon.

I lift my head up and look around me. I don't know how long I've been sitting here, shivering, when the sun starts to set. "He'll be home soon," I mumble to myself, over and over again. He said he would only be gone an hour or two. He has to be home soon, even if it seems like he's running a little bit late. As the sun completely disappears beyond the horizon, a snowflake lands on my nose and then another on my cheek and another on my shoulders and knees. Snowflakes begin swirling hard and fast all around me. I look around, my mouth dropped open in shock. I exhale a humorless laugh, as I stare up into the sky. "Are you kidding me?" I challenge, almost desperately. I glare up at the snow, more than cold at this point and completely exhausted.

I pull the boxes close to me, building as much of a barrier from the wind and the snow as possible, hoping to keep myself dry. I wish I had something else to help protect me, but I don't, so this is the best I can do. I grimace and wrap my arms around my knees again, tucking my head in close. "Chris, please come home," I whisper, between my chattering teeth. "I need you," I whimper. I start fighting to stay awake, forcing my eyes to open every time they close. Eventually, my eyes flutter closed, without my consent, with my whole body feeling numb. I'm only able to maintain my focus on one thing and that's staying as warm as possible until Chris comes for me. "Chris," I softly murmur his name, as I fall into a deep sleep.

Chapter 16

Chris

I pull into a parking lot with a small strip of stores. I park in front of a one-level tan building with white trim. There's a lime green sign in front of the first shop with, "Franz Music Studio" written in large, red lettering and underneath, a little smaller in yellow it states, "Piano, Guitar, Voice & Musical Theatre." I step out of my SUV and onto the cement walkway, leading to the front door. I pass by an older man with gray hair, who is sitting on a wooden bench with a young girl, about 6 or 7 years old with long, dark brown wavy hair. She's talking animatedly to him as her legs swing back and forth, while he looks down at her, obviously enamored. She must be his granddaughter. I pull the front door open and step inside, closing the door behind me.

A pretty woman, standing behind the counter looks up at me as I enter. She startles, as if surprised, but if it's Bella, she knew I was coming, so that can't be why. "You must be Christian Ackerman," she proclaims, as she approaches me with a wide smile.

My eyebrows draw down in question and I mumble, "Bella?" needing clarification. She's wearing black leggings, simple black shoes and a cream, vertically ribbed, turtleneck sweater.

She grins and nods her head in confirmation. "That's me," she announces. "It's very nice to meet you," she declares.

139

She steps into my space and wraps her arms around me in a hug, taking me by surprise. "Oh! Ah, hi," I stammer, awkwardly returning her embrace.

"Merry has told me so much about you," she informs me.

My heart skips a beat with her comment and I quickly try to brush it off. "All good, I hope," I reply, with a crooked smile.

She grins and reveals, "I haven't heard her talk about how much she loves a job in," she pauses, thinking, "Well, ever!"

My heart sinks and my shoulders sag, although I try to hide my disappointment. Of course, it's about the job, not me. "Oh, the job?" I question. "That's great," I mumble, forcing a smile.

Bella looks me over carefully, assessing me. Then she quickly amends, "I mean, she speaks very highly of you, too."

My heart skips a beat and I narrow my eyes, feeling hopeful. "Really?" I prompt, hoping she's not just placating me.

She bites her lower lip, as if fighting a smile and nods her head in confirmation. "Yes. I'm actually surprised we never met before," she divulges.

I nod in acknowledgement and explain, "I never went further than Christmas Cove when I came for the holidays or summers. My grandparents had everything we really needed right there, you know?" I prompt.

"Totally," she agrees, nodding her head. "Family time, right?"

"Exactly," I affirm.

"So," she begins, "what can I help you with?" she probes.

I gesture to the chairs and cushioned benches sitting up against the walls, around the front of the room.

"Can we sit for a little while?" I propose. "This might take longer than a couple of minutes, hence why I made an appointment," I elaborate.

"Sure," she agrees. "We can sit here," she offers, gesturing to a bench against the wall, underneath the painted name of the studio.

She sits on one end and waits for me. I slip my coat off and cautiously sit down, setting my coat next to me, as I think about what I want to say. I take a deep breath and just blurt it out, knowing there's no easy way to say this. "Merry told me that she has been spending the holidays with you and your family since you two were twelve," I announce.

She straightens almost instantly and her eyes widen in surprise. "Oh, so she really has talked about me," she concedes.

I nod my head and smile, thinking about how Merry described her best friend. "Yeah, she has. She loves you like a sister," I reveal, although, I'm sure she already knows.

She smiles fondly at my statement and I can't help, but like her for that reaction alone. "Aw, I feel the same way about her," she confesses.

"How about you come to Christmas at my house?" I propose.

She huffs a surprised laugh. "Wow, that's very sweet of you. But, I'm spending Christmas with my family," she proclaims.

"Invite them," I insist. I know Meredith would want all of them to be there if it were possible. That way, she can spend Christmas with Bella and her family like she does nearly every year. I want her to be surrounded by the people she loves.

She arches her eyebrows in challenge. "All of them?" she pushes.

141

I shrug like it's no big deal, as the corners of my mouth curve upwards, feeling good about this decision. "Yeah," I concur. "Why not?"

"You're talking about seven people and a baby," she clarifies and continues to elaborate. "Me, my mom, my dad, my brother Brian, his wife Lauren, their baby, my little sister Jessica, my..."

I interrupt because right now, their names don't matter. They are all welcome. "Can you talk to them and find out if they're okay with it?"

"Sure," she replies. "But Christmas is in three days," she reminds me. "I'm sure they've already started preparing dinner."

"So, bring it," I suggest, knowing that will help Meredith. She's already doing so much. "The more food, the better. Right?" I prompt, my smile growing.

"Okay," she smiles, obviously shocked by my offer. "I'll text you," she states.

I nod in acknowledgement and then I quickly continue, before I lose my nerve. "That's not all," I divulge.

"Okay," she replies, dragging out the word.

I take a deep breath and exhale slowly, knowing I'm about to broach an extremely touchy subject. I steel my nerves and force out the question, "What's up with her parents?"

She has a quick intake of breath as her whole body instantly stiffens. She appears to be slightly taken aback by my question. "What do you mean?" she prods, hesitantly.

I wince, not completely sure what her instant reaction means for Meredith. I quietly admit, "I feel bad for her."

"There's nothing to feel bad about," she states, defensively.

I press my lips tightly together in thought, not quite sure how to explain what I'm feeling and the pain I've seen in her eyes when she talks about spending so much time away from her parents, especially for the holidays. I take another deep breath and exhale slowly, before I try again. "Well, you've seen her deal with that situation her entire life. She just doesn't seem to have any sort of closure," I conclude.

"Can you blame her?" she probes, irritably. She obviously has a lot of resentment regarding the situation on Meredith's behalf. "She doesn't exist to them!" she exclaims, vehemently.

I grimace at her outburst, my heart clenching tightly for Meredith. "They're her parents," I reiterate, emphatically. I want to try to do something to help. I need to.

"So?" she prompts. "Not everyone has a cozy, close relationship with their parents. Some people don't have a relationship at all," she announces, defensively.

I sigh heavily and nod in understanding. "It just seems like Meredith really wants one," I explain, revealing my motivation to do something to help.

Bella flinches and nods sadly. "She does," she concedes.

"I want to invite them for Christmas," I enlighten her.

She shakes her head and declares, "They won't come. I'm telling you right now, they will turn you down and you do not want Meredith to be around them if she's hosting your Christmas dinner. She'll be a mess," she emphasizes.

I sigh and concede, "Fair enough." I pause, trying to think of another option, when suddenly an idea pops into my head. "What about Christmas Eve dinner? Maybe I can call them and invite them here," I suggest.

"I'll give you their phone number," she offers, "but you're wasting your breath," she claims, bitterly.

My heart clenches, my chest aching at her reaction, knowing it's a result of watching Meredith go through so much pain over the years. I hate that for her. I take a deep breath, feeling even more determined. I grin at Bella with a feeling of determination. "I can be very convincing," I proclaim.

She smirks and responds, "I'm sure." She holds her hand out to me, palm up. Then she requests, "Give me your phone."

I reach into my pocket and pull it out. I open it up and pull up my contacts. I add a new contact and then I hand her my phone. She begins typing the information into my phone. I smile gratefully and mumble, "Thank you."

Bella purses her lips in thought as she stares at me, as if trying to read my mind. "Don't say I didn't warn you," she finally grumbles.

I breathe a sigh of relief, knowing she's giving me a chance to help Meredith. "I know. I appreciate it," I tell her, sincerely.

She glances at me and then focuses back on the phone. "How are you going to get her to cook dinner for four people?" she asks, curiously.

I shake my head and proclaim, "I'm not. I was just thinking I would set up a dinner for them at a restaurant. I can pick them up from the airport and meet her there," I explain.

She hands me back my phone and smiles at me, with a look in her eyes I can't quite decipher. "That's very sweet, Chris. Merry loves surprises. That would really make her Christmas," she reveals, bringing a smile to my face. I don't want to get ahead of myself though. Let's see if I can make it happen first.

"You think?" I prompt.

She nods and confidently answers, "Yes." She swiftly wipes the smile from her face and narrows her eyes, giving me a look of warning, "But don't tell her anything about it. I don't want her getting her hopes up," she asserts.

I nod my head in understanding. The last thing I would want is for Meredith to get her heart broken over this, when all I want to do is to help her. "I won't," I promise.

She offers me a grateful smile. "I'll text you about Christmas," she reiterates. "Thanks for the invitation."

"You're welcome," I reply. "Hopefully, I'll see you there."

She tilts her head to the side and prods, "Is that everything?"

I chuckle softly and nod my head in affirmation. I put my hands on my knees and push, as I stand up. "Yes," I confirm. I pick my coat up off the bench and slip it on. "Thank you. I really appreciate it, Bella," I maintain, truly thankful.

"You're welcome," she responds. She turns back towards the register, as I turn for the front door. "Hey," she calls out, stopping me in my tracks.

I spin back towards her and find her staring intently at me. I arch my eyebrows in question and probe, "Yeah?"

Her eyes turn serious, as she requests, practically pleading, "Don't hurt her."

I grin, thinking about Meredith's smile and how much I truly love having her around. "I wouldn't dream of it," I proclaim.

Bella smiles in response and gives me a look of approval. At least that's how I'm reading her look. "Good," she murmurs softly, under her breath.

I walk out the front door and then close it behind me. I stride out to my car, a small smile on my face, with Meredith on my mind. I slip in behind the wheel and buckle my seat belt. I start the car and slowly back out, anxious to get back to the house to see Merry, even though I haven't been gone very long. I just can't help it. It's like she's turned my whole world around. I pull onto the road, and turn up the radio, as Deck the Halls comes through the speakers. I chuckle to myself, the song another thing that reminds me of her. I sing along, with a small smile on my face.

Chapter 17

Chris

I turn the radio down, as I notice a fire truck up ahead, with its lights flashing and parked horizontally, completely blocking the road leading towards the bridge that crosses over into Christmas Cove. I slow down and roll my window down. I pull to a stop, as a fireman, dressed in full gear, places himself in front of my car and holds his hands out to stop me as he slowly approaches my car. His black helmet has the number 3 in white and the name, "Captain Jack" written on it in red. I glance at the fire engine behind him and notice the same name is painted on the driver's side door of the large red and white fire engine. He walks around to the side of my car and steps towards me, still maintaining his awareness of the traffic around him.

I turn towards him and lean my head out the window. "What's going on?" I inquire, hoping everything is okay.

"The bridge is closed," Captain Jack, announces, his voice firm.

I wince. That's the only way to get to and from Christmas Cove without a boat. "What? Why?" I prompt. I'm suddenly anxious, thinking about not being able to get home to Meredith.

"Bad accident on both sides," he reveals. "We're just waiting on the tow truck and then we'll do a quick cleanup before we'll be able to open it back up," he informs me.

"Any idea how long it could be?" I question.

He shakes his head and shrugs his shoulders. "No idea," he replies, honestly. Then he suggests, "If you want, there's a strip mall over there," he points over my car and I turn around to see where he's gesturing. I notice a small strip of about three or four shops and turn back to him. "You'll be able to watch traffic from the coffee shop," he advises.

Well, I guess that's better than sitting on the side of the road. I force a smile, knowing it's not his fault. "Thanks," I murmur.

"Yup," he responds and nods his head in acknowledgement. Then he steps back from my car and waves me on.

I roll up my window as I make a U-turn and immediately pull into the strip mall. I park right in front of the coffee shop and sigh heavily as I turn off my car. "Hopefully this won't take long," I grumble under my breath.

I unbuckle my seat belt and step out of my car, closing the door behind me. The glass front doors of the coffee shop are bordered with windows on both sides and the top. I pull the door open and step inside, the atmosphere bright. I glance over the glass cases of treats and continue on to the front counter. A man with the nametag, "Casey," stands behind the counter with a welcoming smile.

"Hi! What can I get you?" he inquires, politely.

I glance up at the menu one more time before I reply, "A hot chocolate would be great." There's a chill in the air, as if it's about to snow. Something warm while I wait is exactly what I need right now.

"Marshmallows and whipped cream?" he questions.

"Sure," I reply. I grin, my mouth already watering for the unexpected treat.

He taps the cash register in front of him and then looks up at me. "That will be three-twenty-five," he informs me.

I reach into my back pocket and grab my wallet. I open it up and pull out a five-dollar bill. I hand it to him and paste a smile on my face. "Keep the change," I offer, with a nod of my head.

His grin grows and he murmurs, "Thanks. If you want to grab a table, I'll bring it over to you," he proposes.

"Thank you," I answer. I grab a map from the plastic display holder on the counter and turn around. I walk back towards the front of the shop and stop at a small table. I slip my coat off and hang it over the back of the chair, before I sit down. I glance out the window one more time before I open the map and look it over. I want to know the area better, now that I'll be spending even more time here in Maine. I guess this is as good a time as any.

Casey approaches me with my cup of hot chocolate in hand. "Here you are," he offers holding it out to me.

"Oh," I stammer. I quickly fold the map back up and set it aside, getting it out of the way, before I reach up and take the cup from him. "Thank you," I mumble, with a polite smile. He nods his head in acknowledgement, before he turns and walks away. I slowly take a sip, careful not to burn my lips or tongue. I pause, closing my eyes as I enjoy the thick, creamy, sweet, chocolate taste as it runs over my tongue and down my throat. I open my eyes as I set the cup down on the table in front of me, with a sigh of satisfaction.

I reach into my coat pocket and pull my cell phone out. I unlock the screen and open my text messages. I click on Meredith's name and tap out a quick message. "There was an accident on the bridge. Looks like I'm going to be delayed here for a little while. Not sure how long. I'll grab us some pizza for dinner on the way home. Let me know what you like on your pizza. I'll text when I'm on my way," I add.

I take another sip of my hot chocolate, when my phone rings and my best friend's face lights up the screen. I tap answer and declare, "Hi, Jordan!"

"Hey, Chris," he rasps, hoarsely.

I wince at the strained sound of his voice. "You don't sound too good," I mutter.

He chuckles humorlessly. "I'm sure I don't look too good either," he concedes.

I sigh in disappointment. "I guess that means you're not going to be able to come for Christmas," I state.

"I'm really sorry Chris. We were looking forward to it," he informs me.

"I understand," I murmur. "Well, maybe next year," I add.

"Yeah. That would be great," he mumbles.

"Feel better, Jordan," I encourage.

"Thanks. Merry Christmas," he declares.

"Merry Christmas," I proclaim. "Tell your family the same from me, too," I remind him.

"I will and you too," he requests.

"Of course. Get some rest," I insist.

"Bye," he replies.

I disconnect the call and lift my cup to my lips, taking another drink. Then, I quickly scroll to find the phone number Bella just entered into my phone for me. I should make the call now while Meredith's not around. I would hate to have her overhear and then have it not work out the way she would like. I tap the number and wait for the line to connect.

"Karl Block," he announces, professionally.

I take a deep breath and introduce myself as I exhale. "Hello, Dr. Block. My name is Christian Ackerman," I announce.

"Who?" he prods, sounding confused.

"Christian Ackerman," I repeat.

"Do I know you?" he inquires, before I have a chance to say anything more.

"No, Sir," I shake my head, even though he can't see me. "Not yet," I add, hopeful. "I know your daughter, Meredith," I quickly explain.

"Is everything alright?" he prompts, suddenly sounding worried.

"Yes, of course," I instantly reply to calm his anxiety. "No need for alarm," I emphasize. Although, his concern does give me hope. "I actually hired Meredith to work for me this month," I enlighten him.

"Oh, so you are her boss," he concludes, as understanding sinks in. "How is that going?" he probes.

"Very well, Dr. Block," I reply, honestly. "Your daughter is immensely talented," I compliment her. I feel as if I could say so much more, but I don't think now is the time.

"Thank you. Her mother and I are very proud of her," he declares. The pride in his voice is obvious, taking me by surprise.

"Really?" I prompt.

"Well, of course," he confirms, defensively. "She went to an ivy league college for her Bachelors in business," he brags. "Now, running her own business puts that to excellent use," he elaborates.

I grimace, happy with his answer, but also knowing I can't let it go that easy. She deserves more. "Have you ever told her that?" I push.

"Excuse me?" he questions, obviously offended.

"Mr. Block, I'll be frank with you," I begin. I'm determined for him to understand and I can only hope it will be enough to make a difference. "Meredith misses you. She wants a relationship with you and she doesn't know how to go about having that relationship," I reveal. I pause, waiting for a response from him, but the line remains silent. "Dr. Block?" I prompt. I hope I'm reading him correctly and this will make a difference. The last thing I want to do would be to make things harder on her. "Are you still there?" I prod.

I hear him move around on the other end of the line and clear his throat, before he finally speaks. "Please, call me Karl," he requests.

"She told me that your wife is working on Christmas," I state.

"Yes, she is," he confirms.

"Is she also working Christmas Eve?" I question.

"No. Neither of us are working," he clarifies. "Why?" he probes.

I take another deep breath, hoping this works. "How would you feel about taking a quick trip to Maine for an early dinner?" I propose.

"I think that's a great idea and I'm almost positive we could make that work," he responds, confidently.

"Great," I reply. I feel my whole body sag with relief, as a smile tugs at my lips.

We quickly work through the details. After we hang up, he texts me back only a few minutes later with their confirmation, after speaking with his wife. I finish up the particulars, confirming a flight, as well as restaurant reservations for three for tomorrow night, while I wait for traffic to finally start to move across the road. I glance out the window and sigh at the setting sun, watching as day quickly turns to night. It gets dark so early here in the winter. I lift my cup and swallow the last of the hot chocolate.

Casey walks around, going from table to table and talking to customers. He approaches me and notices my empty mug. He picks it up and prompts, "Need anything else?"

I shake my head in response. "Nah, thanks." I glance out the window and breathe a sigh of relief at the sight of the headlights finally moving over the bridge. "Traffic is moving again," I proclaim, a broad smile on my face.

He turns towards the front of the shop and glances out the windows, nodding his head in affirmation. Then he turns back to me and advises, "Be careful driving across that bridge."

I smile and nod my head in acknowledgement. "Will do," I affirm. "Thanks."

I grab my coat off the back of the chair and pull it on. Then I grab my phone and slip it into my pocket, before I turn and walk out the front door. I pause on the sidewalk, glancing up into the darkened sky at the fresh falling snow. A chill suddenly passes through me and I hurry to my car. I climb in behind the wheel and buckle my seatbelt with a click. My stomach growls, the sound reminding me of my plan. I pull out my phone and grimace when I don't see any response from Meredith, but I'm sure she's just lost in her work as always. I search for the pizza place on Christmas Cove, right next door to the small town market. I smile to myself when I find it and tap the number. Then, I wait to be connected.

"Anthony's Pizza," a man announces.

"Yes, I'd like to order a large cheese pizza for pick-up?" I request.

"Absolutely. Name?" he prompts.

"Christian Ackerman," I reply.

"It will be about twenty minutes," he proclaims.

"Thank you," I respond and disconnect the call.

It will be nice to do something for Meredith for once. It feels like she's always taking care of me. Hopefully she didn't eat yet. I start my car and back out. I slowly make my way back onto the road, turning towards Christmas Cove. With freshly fallen snow on the ground, I tap the breaks, testing them to see how slick the roads are. I sigh and drive with caution, wanting to get home safe.

Chapter 18

Chris

I pull into the driveway and park my car next to the garage, like always. I turn off the car and unbuckle my seat belt, before I grab the pizza, sitting next to me on the passenger seat. I climb out of the car and walk around back. I pull the sliding glass door open and step into the dark house. I stomp the snow off my boots right by the door, not wanting to track it through the house. "Merry? I'm home," I call, but she doesn't respond.

I stride into the darkened kitchen and flip on the light. I set the pizza down on the dining room table, as I look around, hearing nothing but silence. Then I slip my coat off and hang it over the back of the chair, while I call for her again. "Merry? I brought pizza," I yell, hoping to pull her from whatever she's working on. "I'm sorry. It took me a lot longer than I expected. There was an accident on the bridge," I explain, loudly.

I turn and saunter towards the foyer, worry starting to gnaw at me. "Merry?" I repeat. I step towards the stairs and call up, "Meredith?" My own voice echoes back at me with no response or even a sound from Merry. "Where are you?" I mumble under my breath.

My heart suddenly drops into the pit of my stomach as realization of what she was doing just before I left hits me like a freight train. I gasp and sprint up the stairs, taking them two at a time. I fly into the master bedroom and spot her slumped over against the railing, outside on the balcony. I can barely breathe as I bound through the room and throw the sliding glass door open.

155

"Merry," I yell as I quickly prop the door open. "Meredith," I call, her name a desperate plea on my lips.

I bend down and pick her up, cradling her in my arms. She feels so cold. I pull her close to my chest and rush her inside. I set her down carefully on the bed and throw a blanket over her. I make sure the door is closed tight and sit down next to her. I rest my hand on her ice-cold cheek and take in her appearance. Her skin is pale blue and her lips are so dark, they have a bluish-purple hue to them. "Merry! Meredith! Say something," I plead, urgently. "Merry," I repeat, frantically, struggling for breath.

"S...S...So c...c...cold," she stutters, without opening her eyes.

I run to the spare bedroom, across the hall and grab the thick comforter off the bed. I rush back into the room and quickly cover her up with it. I reach under the bottom of the blanket and slip off her damp shoes and socks. "You gotta' dry off Merry. You gotta' get warm," I beg. My hands envelop her frozen toes and I gasp in shock. I run back into the spare bedroom and open up the top drawer of the dresser, remembering where we keep the extra thick, fuzzy socks. I grab the first pair I see and hurry back to Meredith. I gently pull them on her feet and then cover her back up with the blanket and comforter.

I kneel down next to the bed and hold her hand in mine, rubbing it, gentle, but firm in attempt to warm her up. "Come on Meredith," I implore. "Merry. Meredith. Merry," I whisper her name over and over again, like it's my mantra, while I try to warm her up. "Come on, Merry."

My cell phone rings and I quickly glance at the screen. I see my boss's name, Larry Link and instantly decline the call. I flip my phone to silent, before I toss it on the nightstand, not caring about anything, but Meredith. She's all that matters.

I hold Merry's hand as I talk to her, pleading with her to be okay. "Merry, I'm so sorry. I told you to prop the door open," I voice, as if I can stop this from happening. I shouldn't have left when she was going out there. This is my fault. "You'll be okay," I declare, attempting to convince both of us it's true. "I'm trying to get you warm," I whisper, as I rub her arms. "Merry," I rasp her name, my whole body aching with fear.

I slip my shoes off and sit down next to her on the bed. I carefully wrap my arm around her and hold her close. Her cheek falls to my chest, as I continue rubbing her arms and back, trying to warm her up any way I can. I brush her hair away from her face and look down at her adoringly. She has to be okay.

I don't know how long we're sitting there, when her skin no longer feels cold to my touch, but she still doesn't open her eyes. I glance at her and notice her normal color returning to her face. I look at her fingers and see the same. I attempt to gulp down the lump in my throat, feeling completely overwhelmed with emotion. I need a moment to pull myself together. I take a deep breath and carefully ease Meredith out from under my arm and onto the pillow. I slowly slip off the bed, not wanting to disturb her after what she just went through. I look down at her, carefully brushing her hair away from her face. My chest aches, sending painful tingles throughout my body and originating in my heart, where it hurts the most.

I force myself to step out of the room and make my way downstairs to the kitchen. I put on some water for tea, to calm my nerves and hopefully warm her even more when she wakes. She will wake up. She has to. The whistle on the kettle blows and I immediately remove it

157

from the burner. I pour the water into a black mug and set it down next to the sink, allowing it to steep. I lean my hands on the sink and look out the back window, the full moon shining down on the lake.

"Grandpa," I whisper, "you gotta help me out here," I plead. "She's gotta' be okay. When I look at her, I see what you and Grandma had together," I claim. "For the first time in my life, I want something more than a successful career. I want what you had. I want a family. I want love," I confess. "Please, Grandpa. Please wake her up," I beg, desperately. I sigh heavily and drop my head, feeling defeated, as I focus on just breathing in and out.

"Chris?" Meredith calls, her voice a harsh whisper.

My head snaps up at the sound. I immediately spin on my heel and sprint upstairs. I rush into the room and breathe a sigh of relief at the sight of Meredith sitting up in bed. Her blue eyes are open and she looks up at me in confusion. "What happened?" she prompts.

I dive towards her and throw my arms around her. "You're okay," I rasp, the only words I'm able to get out. I hold her tight, not wanting to let her go. Her arms slowly come around me and I finally begin to relax, as my heartbeat begins to slow. She's still confused, but I need a moment just to hold her, knowing she's going to be okay, before I can explain what happened.

"I'm okay," she murmurs, repeating me.

I sigh and slowly release her. Her hands fall to her lap. "You really scared me, Meredith," I confess.

"I'm sorry," she whispers.

I shake my head and insist, "Don't apologize. I'm just glad you're okay." I stand, remembering the tea. "I just made some tea. Let me bring you a cup," I offer. "It will help you warm up from the inside, out."

She nods in acknowledgement and murmurs, "Thanks."

"I'll be right back," I declare. I rush back to the kitchen and pull out a white mug with a red heart painted on it. I pour the tea and bring it upstairs, with the tea bag still inside, but I don't have the patience to wait at the moment.

"Here," I offer, as I step up to the bed.

She sits a little taller before accepting the cup. "Thank you," she mumbles. Her fingers lightly brush mine in the exchange and I relax a little more at the warmth of her touch. I watch as she carefully takes a small sip and then leans towards the nightstand with the cup.

I swiftly reach in to assist her. "Here, let me help," I offer. I grasp the mug and set it down for her. "You really scared me, Meredith. I'm so sorry I wasn't here. There was an accident on the bridge," I begin.

She shakes her head and interrupts me. "It was an accident," she declares, still sounding a little shaky. "I propped the door open, but it must've slipped," she explains.

I grimace. "I'm just glad you're okay," I reiterate because it's worth repeating. "How are you feeling?" I prompt.

She winces slightly, and then admits, "I still have a little chill. I'll be okay to go home though."

My eyes widen and I shake my head in refusal. "You're not going anywhere," I insist. Her eyes widen in shock and I quickly continue, before she can argue with me. "You can sleep here tonight. There's plenty of room. You know there is. You're already comfortable and I'll sleep in one of the other bedrooms tonight," I offer. "Besides, after what you just went through today, someone should be checking on you regularly tonight to make sure you don't spike a fever or something. I can do that for you," I propose. "Please, let me do that for you?" I request, emphatically.

She stares into my eyes, as if trying to read my mind. "Okay," she relents. I breathe a sigh of relief. "I need to call Bella and ask her to go to my place to feed Thaddeus for me," she informs me.

I flinch and watch her reaction as I admit, "I already texted her."

"Really?" she questions.

I nod in confirmation, "Yeah. I hope you don't mind."

She offers me a small smile. "No, not at all. Thank you," she mumbles. "I can sleep in one of the other rooms, though. I don't want to take your bed."

I shake my head, "No, stay here. Please," I beg. "You're already comfortable. Plus, I'm not even used to sleeping in here yet," I claim. She gives me a crooked smile and my heart skips a beat. I clear my throat and suggest, "If you want to change into something more comfortable to sleep in, you can have something of mine from the dresser."

"Thank you," she murmurs, appreciatively.

"Is there anything else I can do for you?" I question. "I can help with whatever you need tomorrow too," I proclaim.

"I think I have everything taken care of. Besides, finishing up out there," she smirks.

I huff a humorless laugh and shake my head. "I won't be going anywhere when you're here," I announce. "I don't want you to overdo anything," I emphasize

She nods her head in acknowledgement. Then, she continues, revealing, "I just have to start preparing all of the dishes tomorrow and Christmas Eve."

"About Christmas Eve," I begin.

"Yes?" she prompts.

"Would you like to have dinner with me?" I request, my heart pounding in anticipation.

Her eyebrows draw down in confusion, since we've spent every meal together the last few weeks. "Do you want me to cook?" she asks.

I shake my head, "No, not at all. I thought we could go to that Italian restaurant in town," I propose.

"Oh, I've actually never been there," she murmurs.

"I'd love to take you," I tell her, honestly. "Unless you have other plans," I mutter, anxiously. I don't know what I'll do, if she says she has plans.

She shakes her head and replies, "No, I don't have any plans. I'd love to go," she proclaims, causing me to smile wide.

"Great!" I declare, feeling the tension release from my shoulders. "I made reservations for five o'clock," I broadcast.

She laughs, the sound sending tingles down my spine. "A little sure of yourself, huh?" she teases me.

I feel my face heat instantly. I can't help but wish this really was a date, but doing this for her is more important than what I want. I shrug and prompt, "Wishful thinking?"

She giggles in response and I smile down at her, my heart feeling full of hope. "Thank you," she states.

My eyebrows draw down in confusion. "For what?" I question.

"For thinking of me," she murmurs, her cheeks turning a beautiful shade of pink. "I would have been alone on Christmas Eve."

My heart lurches, feeling her pain. I quickly gulp down the lump in my throat, knowing I've done the right thing. If I could help it, she would never feel that kind of pain again. "Oh, that reminds me," I begin, swiftly changing the subject. "We need to add ten more to Christmas Day," I state.

Her eyes widen in shock. "Ten?" she repeats.

I grimace at her reaction, hoping it's not too much. I don't want to put too much pressure on her, especially after what she just went through today. "Is that okay?" I probe, anxiously. "I have some other family that wanted to come. They're going to be bringing some food too," I elaborate, hoping that helps.

She nods her head in acceptance, "Okay." She pauses and then confirms, "Ten is no problem. We'll need a couple more tables, though," she reminds me.

I nod my head in understanding, grateful for her easygoing demeanor. "I have them in the garage," I inform her.

"Then you can definitely help me set them up tomorrow," she instructs.

I grin, happy to do anything I can to help her. "Great," I affirm.

She yawns, quickly covering her mouth with her hand. "I think I'm ready to go to sleep," she mumbles.

"I don't blame you. It's one in the morning," I reveal.

Her mouth drops open in shock and she mutters, "No! Is it?"

I nod my head in confirmation. "Yeah. No alarms tomorrow, okay?" I request. She opens her mouth as if to argue. "Just sleep in. Your body needs it," I insist.

She grimaces, realizing it's true. "But I have so much to do," she complains.

"I'll help," I reiterate. "Get some sleep. That's an order from your boss," I joke.

She arches her eyebrows in surprise and grins. "Yes, Sir," she concurs.

I smile down at her, already looking so much better and I breathe another sigh of relief. "Goodnight, Meredith," I murmur.

"Goodnight, Chris," she replies.

I turn and reluctantly walk out of the room, pulling the door closed behind me. I stand just outside the door and close my eyes. I'm incredibly grateful she's going to be okay. I huff a humorless laugh and admit to myself that's a massive understatement. My heart clenches tightly in my chest and I whisper under my breath, "Thanks, Grandpa."

Chapter 19

Meredith

I twist the sides of my hair and connect them in a low ponytail in the back of my head. I unwillingly let a few loose curls fall out in the front. I want to try to keep my hair out of my face, knowing I'll be in the kitchen for most of the day, but I also want to look good. I grab my lipstick and remove the cap, before I glide it over my lips and swiftly rub them together, as I replace the top. I glance in the mirror hanging on the back of Chris's bathroom door, taking one more look at myself. Bella brought me over some of my things, including a toothbrush, some deodorant, and a bag with clean clothes for me to wear, as well as a few other necessary items. I'm wearing a cherry red turtleneck sweater, black leggings and short black boots. I run my hand over my clothes, smoothing out a few wrinkles, before I open the door. I fold my clothes from yesterday and put them in the bag Bella brought for me and set it down by the bedroom door. I'll have to remember to put it in my car later, but for now I'll just leave it here, so it's out of the way.

I step out of the bathroom and make my way downstairs. I walk into the kitchen, finding Bella sitting at the counter, sipping her coffee, while she waits for me. "Bella, thank you, so much!" I croon, as I stride directly for the coffee pot.

She looks up at me from behind the cream coffee mug decorated with a moose in a Santa hat and smiles at me. "I'm happy to help," she responds. "Honestly, I'm just really glad you're feeling better," she emphasizes. "I can't believe you were stuck outside for so long," she murmurs. She grimaces and shakes her head in disbelief.

I press my lips tightly together and finish pouring my coffee. I fight a shiver running down my spine and remind myself I'm okay. Everyone has worried about me enough and saying too much will bring back their concern when I'm ready to move on. I know better now. I replace the pot and walk over to the refrigerator. I pull the door open and reach for the creamer. I open it and pour a little into my mug, before immediately returning it to the refrigerator and closing the door. Then, I make my way to the other side of the counter and sit down on the stool next to Bella. She looks amazing, like always, wearing a long, cream, cable-knit sweater with a cowl neck, paired with dark brown leggings and tall brown boots. "I'm just really glad Chris got home and found me when he did," I admit, knowing I need to give her something. "But I really do appreciate this, Bella," I emphasize. I gesture to my outfit with a broad smile.

"Of course," she reiterates, as she nods her head in understanding. She swiftly looks me over from head to toe and grins. "You look good," she compliments.

I huff a laugh, wondering if her compliment is because she picked out my clothes. I smirk and mumble, "Thanks."

She chuckles, understanding my amusement and nods in acknowledgment. "I stopped by your house again this morning and fed Thaddeus," she enlightens me. She knows how much I worry about him when I'm gone for a long time.

"Really?" I prod, with wide eyes.

"Yes," she confirms, nodding her head. Then she takes a sip of her coffee and sets it down on the counter.

I breathe a sigh of relief, knowing I have one less thing to think about. "You're the best!" I announce, praising her.

I notice Chris saunter into the kitchen from the corner of my eye. I reflexively turn my head towards him, my heart skipping a beat at the sight. He stretches, reaching his arms above his head, his usually perfectly styled hair, slightly mussed from sleep. He's wearing navy blue and white flannel pajama bottoms with a gray t-shirt, obviously just waking up. He rubs a hand down his face and freezes the instant he spots Bella and me sitting at the kitchen counter. "Good morning," he rumbles, his deep voice not yet awake.

"Morning!" I reply, cheerfully. "Coffee?" I offer.

He nods his head in response and requests, "Please."

I stand up and quickly walk around the counter towards the coffee pot. A slightly confused look crosses over his features, as he glances from me to Bella and then back to me. "Oh, I'm sorry," I stammer, shaking my head. "Chris, this is my best friend, Bella. I've told you about her," I remind him, introducing the two of them.

He nods his head in recognition and grins. "Right. Hi," he adds, politely. He takes a step towards her, with his hand outstretched.

She rises to meet him halfway. She holds her hand out to him and shakes it. "Nice to meet you," she claims, greeting him, with an almost over-zealous smile.

"Likewise," Chris replies, the corners of his mouth twitching upwards. His smile grows as he drops his hands to his sides. My stomach twists anxiously at their exchange. A feeling of jealousy nearly overwhelms me, my heart tightening in my chest, making it difficult to breathe. I did tell her I wasn't interested in him, I remind myself. I take a deep breath and attempt to gulp down the lump in my throat. I open the cabinet and grab a white mug, with red and white candy canes crisscrossing one another on the front. I close the cabinet and reach for the half empty coffee pot and pour Chris a cup, before returning the pot to the burner.

"Well, I've got to go, Merry," Bella announces. She picks up her bronze colored winter coat, with a thick olive green lining and quickly slips it on. "Today is the last day before Christmas break, so I need to make sure no instruments were left behind before I close up for the next week and a half," she informs me.

I nod my head in understanding, knowing she always closes for the holidays. "Leave your cup on the counter," I instruct. "I'll take care of it."

"Thanks," she murmurs.

"Well, I'll call you when I get home tonight," I advise.

"Sounds good," she murmurs, nodding in agreement. I spin around with the coffee cup for Chris in my hand and step towards him, just as Bella turns her focus on him. "Thanks for rescuing her," she tells him, gratefully.

Chris smiles and nods in acknowledgement. "You don't have to thank me," he insists. "I'm happy I got here when I did," he concedes, sincerely. He glances down at me as I hand him his black coffee, his look adoring. I feel my cheeks heat almost instantly, as my heart begins to race.

I tear my gaze away from him and take a small step away, needing a little space between us as I look up at Bella. "Bye, Bella," I grin. She returns my smile, her eyes sparkling with delight and amusement. She waves as she turns and walks out of the room, towards the front door. I try not to read into her look, but I'm sure she'll tell me all about it later anyway.

167

I wait until I hear the front door close behind her, before I speak. "I hope you don't mind that she came by this morning," I grimace. "I needed some fresh clothes and a few other things for today," I reveal.

He gives me a crooked smile and shakes his head, waving me off, like it's no big deal. "No, not at all," he proclaims.

"I wanted to get an early start on prepping all of the food," I elaborate. I'm glad I thought to send a text to her last night, before I fell asleep to ask for her help. Otherwise, I'd be wearing yesterday's clothes. I just don't have time to run home this morning after losing so much time yesterday. I have way too much to do.

He nods in understanding. "Need any help?" he inquires.

"With the food?" I question. I shake my head and reply without waiting for his answer. "No, but I'll need help with the tables and chairs. The ones you said your grandpa has somewhere," I add, as a reminder.

"Great," he proclaims, nodding his head in agreement. "Just give me a shout when you need them and I'll take care of it," he requests.

I smile appreciatively and murmur my acknowledgement, "Okay, thanks."

He purses his lips and his eyebrows suddenly draw down in concern, as he takes a small step closer to me. "How are you feeling this morning?" he prompts.

I give him a reassuring smile and emphatically insist, "I'm feeling so much better, Chris. Thank you," I repeat. He opens his mouth as if to argue or push the issue more, but I don't want to keep talking about it. I'm embarrassed I locked myself out in the first place, even if I am more than grateful he rescued me. I look into his eyes, as I step a little closer to him and lay my hand gently on his forearm. I interrupt, before he can say anything else and emphasize, "Really."

He looks me over, as if checking to make sure himself. Then he finally offers me a crooked smile and nods his head in acceptance. "Good," he mumbles, sounding relieved. "Did you sleep okay?" he questions.

I nod my head and let my hand fall to my side. "I slept great," I answer, truthfully. I don't know if it was because of everything that happened or because of how hard I've been working, but I was completely exhausted. Maybe it was comforting to know that Chris was close by if I needed him, but I'm not about to admit that out loud. "Thank you for letting me stay here," I recognize. He grins and nods his head in acknowledgement.

I pause awkwardly, wanting to change the subject. I do remember there's something I wanted to ask him about Christmas, when it suddenly comes to me. "Chris," I call to get his attention, even though he hasn't moved or even taken his eyes off me. "What do you think of having dinner buffet style?" I propose.

"What do you mean?" he asks, for clarification.

"You have such a beautiful open kitchen and there will be over 20 people here. What if I set up a buffet on the counter with all of the food, instead of putting everything on the tables?" I suggest. "It might be easier for everyone, especially since we'll have more than one table," I add.

He nods his head in agreement, "Yeah, I think that could work. I mean, I need to do some things my own way if this is my house now, right?" He looks at me, with a question in his eyes, as if wanting my approval.

"Right," I confirm, nodding my head in agreement. "New traditions aren't a bad thing," I encourage. "Plus, I think when you mix a little of your old traditions from your grandfather, with some new ones of your own, it feels more personal," I emphasize. He nods his head slowly, as if deep in thought. "And you already have more people coming this year, than just your family," I remind him. "Right?" I prompt.

He grins and nods his head in acceptance. "Right," he confirms, his eyes glinting mischievously, but I don't ask him to explain. He looks down at me, his eyes turning serious, before he adds, "And I have you here too." Butterflies take flight in my stomach, as I feel my face instantly turn beet red. I step back towards the counter, not sure how to respond. I reach for my coffee cup, taking another sip, just for something to do. "I need to get some work done," he announces, swiftly changing the subject. "I'll be in the game room if you need me," he enlightens me.

I look up at him and paste a smile on my face as I nod my head in response. "Okay. I'll be in the kitchen all day," I apprise him. "I won't bother you," I add. I'm sure he's busy finishing up some of his year-end work before the holidays begin tomorrow.

He gasps at my comment and his look instantly turns intense. He momentarily holds my gaze, as if willing me to understand, or believe him, or maybe both. Then, he firmly declares, "You're never a bother, Meredith."

Surprised by him, I have a sharp intake of breath as my heart skips a beat. I gulp and smile shyly up at him. He returns my smile and nods his head, before he turns and walks away. He heads upstairs towards the bedrooms, probably to get ready for the day first. I take a deep breath and another sip of my coffee, trying to reign myself in. I feel a little out of sorts today with my emotions, but maybe that's just because of what happened to me last night and Chris is the one who saved me. Then again, I haven't been able to get him off my mind since I started working here.

I don't have time to think about it right now. It's almost Christmas. I pull up my list of things I want to do today, under the notes app on my phone. I skim through it, attempting to keep my focus on the Christmas party, by prioritizing everything and putting it in order for today. At the end of the day, I'll reassess, after I see what I have left to do.

Chapter 20

Chris

I walk into the game room, showered and dressed in khaki pants and a simple dark green V-neck sweater, ready for the day. I can't seem to shake the anxious feeling I've had since I found Meredith on the balcony last night, but at least she looks like herself again today and she's incredibly beautiful as always. I don't know what I would've done if something had happened to her. I shake off the chill that runs through me at the thought. I heave a sigh, as I sit down in the leather chair, attempting to push Merry out of the forefront of my thoughts for now. It's hard to get any work done when my thoughts are focused on her.

I pull my laptop into my lap and turn it on. I pull my phone out of my pocket and set it down on the large, round, leather footstool in front of me, so hopefully I'll see the screen light up if anyone calls. I pull up my emails and begin sifting through them, according to priority. My cell phone rings, interrupting my work. I glance at the screen, my boss's name, Larry Link, lighting it up. I set my laptop on the footstool and lean back in the chair as I tap answer and bring the phone to my ear. "Good morning, Larry," I greet him.

"Well, well, well," he grumbles, taking me by surprise. "Look who decided to answer his phone," he mumbles, irritably.

I press my lips tightly together, remembering the numerous missed calls from him last night, but I never had time to get back to him because I was trying desperately to help Merry. She was my priority. "I had an emergency last night," I declare.

"I don't care," he responds, angrily, making me flinch. I bite the inside of my cheek, attempting to hold back my bitter retort. Meredith is definitely more important than answering any phone call. "I called you nine times," he announces.

I take a deep breath, trying to maintain a calm demeanor. "Larry," I begin, "your first call came in after eight," I remind him.

"I'm your boss," he reiterates what we both already know. "You answer whenever I call," he demands.

I shake my head in disbelief, even though he can't see me. "No, I work from nine to five. Last night was the first time in seven years that I didn't answer when you called," I emphasize, reminding him of all my hard work and loyalty over the years.

"You listen to me, Ackerman," he spits out, accusingly. "You working remotely isn't working. You need to get back into the office today," he stresses.

I huff a humorless laugh. "Are you kidding me?" I blurt out, angrily. "I've been putting in more hours working from here, than when I'm in the office!" I declare.

"I need you to be accessible and you clearly are not," he explains, irrationally. He doesn't know what he's talking about.

"That's ridiculous," I grumble.

"Back in the office today, Ackerman," he demands.

I shake my head, completely stunned at his demands. Even if I could make it there to get to the office today, I wouldn't do it. He has no right to ask that of me. "Tomorrow is Christmas Eve," I remind him, bitterly.

"If you don't come back in today, don't come back at all," he states, leaving no room for argument.

He just made this decision incredibly easy for me. I shrug my shoulders, as if it doesn't matter. Then again, it no longer does matter to me. I simply inform him, "Then I'm not coming back." It feels as if a weight is being lifted from my shoulders as I utter the words.

"What?" he gasps, in shock.

"Being up here has made me realize that there is a lot more to life than work," I reply, my thoughts immediately drifting to Meredith. "I quit, Larry," I proclaim.

"If you quit, don't you dare come crawling back to me for a job," he warns.

"I Quit," I emphasize, confidently. A small smile tugs at my lips, as a sense of pride washes over me.

"Ackerman!" he yells, suddenly desperate, but I'm no longer willing to listen to his plea. I've done more than enough for this company over the years. It's time I do what's best for me, even though I'm not exactly sure what that will look like.

"Merry Christmas, Larry!" I proclaim, cheerfully.

I hear him beginning to yell even louder as I tap the red button to disconnect the call. "Acker…" he screams.

I glance at my laptop and close it. There's no need to bother with going through any of my emails or working on the next project now. There no longer is a next project for me anymore. I run my hand down my face, feeling both relieved and satisfied, which tells me I absolutely made the right decision. Then again, all I have to do is think about spending more time with Merry and any remaining doubt will instantly wash away. I smile to myself as I put my hands on my knees and push up to stand as I go in search of Meredith.

I stride into the kitchen and smile at the sight of Meredith standing at the counter, near the sink. She's washing dark, cherry red apples, one at a time. She has the same red, green and white striped apron on, that I've seen her wearing before. She turns around and glances up at me with a question in her eyes. "Hi," she murmurs, sweetly, causing my stomach to flip-flop.

I take a step towards her and request, "Can I help?"

"Really?" she prompts, as she continues washing all the apples and then setting them on a paper towel next to the sink. I smile and nod in confirmation. "You know how to make apple pie?" she inquires, arching her eyebrows in surprise.

I chuckle softly and shrug my shoulders. Then I take a step closer to her and admit, "No." She giggles in response. The sound sending goosebumps up my arms. "Can you teach me?" I propose, taking another step closer to her.

"Sure," she replies. She pauses, narrowing her eyes to look a little closer at me. "But don't you have to work?" she probes.

I grimace, not wanting to talk about my job, or my old job now, for that matter. "I'm taking some time off," I inform her, the corners of my mouth tugging upwards. "Can I help?" I repeat. "Please?" I plead. "I need to start learning to do this stuff on my own, don't I?" I question, arching my eyebrows in challenge.

She stops what she's doing and looks at me with a huge smile on her face, causing my chest to tighten. "Sure," she agrees. "Take your sweater off," she instructs.

My eyebrows draw down in confusion. "Really?" I probe.

She giggles and insists, "Yeah. You don't want to get it dirty," she reminds me. I purse my lips and give her a skeptical look. "Humor me," she requests, the corners of her mouth twitching up in amusement.

I can't say no to her. "Okay," I relent. I reach back with my right hand and pull my sweater off, revealing a gray t-shirt underneath.

She opens a drawer by the stove and pulls out a red and green plaid apron with red ribbons to tie it. "Here," she offers, handing it to me. "Put this on," she commands.

I do as she says, while she turns around to finish cleaning the apples. I slip the ribbon over my head and then tie it around my back. I spot two red silicone oven mitts next to the oven and quickly slip them on my hands, while she still has her back turned. She spins back around and faces me. She stutter steps and immediately catches herself, giggling instantly. I love that sound. "What?" I prod, innocently, holding my hands up in mock offense.

"Okay," she laughs, "now you look a little too domesticated," she teases.

I chuckle in response and pull them off, putting them back where I found them. "So," I grin, "are you going to teach me or what?" I prompt.

"Yeah," she happily agrees, nodding her head in affirmation. "Come here," she encourages. I step up to the counter, right next to her, my heart pounding rapidly. "We'll start with rolling out the pie crust," she informs me. "I already made the dough," she adds. "Wash your hands," she instructs. I do as she says, while she sets up a pastry mat and grabs the dough. This is a much better way to spend my time. I watch as she puts flour on the mat as well as the rolling pin in her hand. Then she hands the rolling pin to me.

"Me?" I prod. She laughs again and nods her head in response. I attempt to roll out the dough, but I can't seem to get it even, no matter what I do.

She giggles and offers to take over. I hand over the rolling pin and watch as she forms a perfect circle, before cutting off the edges with a special tool. She shows me how to pinch the dough along the edges to form the ridges along the edge of the crust. I smile down at her when she nods in agreement, allowing me to finish this one on my own. Although, I did notice this isn't the only one we're making. We continue working together, until we finish the pie. I carefully place it in the oven, next to another one she just placed inside. I close the oven and look back at her with awe. "How did you do that so fast?" I question.

"Practice," she replies, shrugging casually.

I shake my head in amazement and admiration, as we move on to the next pie. She pulls out the food processor and shows me how to use it to make a graham cracker crust for my favorite dessert. "This one is so much easier," I acknowledge.

She laughs and shakes her head in amusement. "I'll make sure to let you do this one next time," she jokes, causing my heart to skip a beat. I like the sound of that. I'm already looking forward to next time with her. She shows me how to make the special chocolate pudding and then I watch as she pours it into the crust.

"What's next?" I inquire.

"How about I finish up here, while you get the tables for me?" I suggest. "Then we can put them where you'd like and I'll set all the tables for Christmas," she informs me.

"I can help set the tables too, if you tell me where you want everything to go," I offer. She smiles back at me, causing my stomach to flip-flop. I reach around my back and untie the apron before I slip it over my head and set it over the stool at the end of the counter. "I'll go get the tables," I announce. I turn around and make my way to the garage, with a huge smile on my face.

We finish the night sitting at the dining room table eating pizza, talking and laughing together. I feel more relaxed tonight than I have in a really long time. I look up and stare into her eyes, truly happy. "Thanks for today, Merry. I really needed it," I emphasize.

"I should be thanking you for all of your help," she reiterates.

"It was fun," I declare, grinning at her like a fool.

She looks at me and gives me a broad smile, completely taking my breath away. "Yeah," she agrees. "It was."

"Can you take tomorrow off?" I request.

She smirks and jokes, "If my boss lets me."

"Go ahead and take off," I insist. "I'm sure you have a lot of your own Christmas stuff you need to get done."

"I do, actually," she acknowledges. "I haven't even gone shopping for Bella and her family," she mumbles, as if she just realized it.

"Are we still on for dinner?" I question. My stomach suddenly twists with nerves, as I await her response.

She smiles and claims, "I wouldn't miss it. Five o'clock, right?" she verifies.

I nod in confirmation, "Yeah."

"Let me help you clean up," she offers and stands up.

I shake my head as I rise. "No, I got it. You go on home," I encourage. "I'm sure Thaddeus misses you," I add, grateful I no longer feel jealous when I hear his name.

"Thanks," she acknowledges. "Good night, Chris," she mumbles, happily, as she pulls her coat on.

"Goodnight, Merry," I murmur. I stand by the table, watching as she walks out the front door. She pulls the door closed behind her and the sound prompts me to start moving. I begin cleaning up the kitchen, as I go over plans for tomorrow in my head. I have to admit, I'm anxious to see her reaction. I hope everything goes well with her parents, but more than anything, I just hope she's happy.

Chapter 21

Meredith

I fold the edges of the red and green Christmas wrapping paper, decorated with Santa and his sleigh in towards the box. "That's the last one," I murmur to myself. I breathe a sigh of relief. I can't believe I waited until Christmas Eve to do all my shopping. Sometimes I have a few last minute gifts, but I've never had to do all of it at the last minute. Then again, I've never had a Christmas client before. I really want to do an incredible job for Chris. I want him to be happy with my work and have a wonderful Christmas with his family. Of course I always want that, but this is different. My stomach twists at the thought of him, reminding me of dinner. I pick up my cell phone and glance at the time. I gasp, "Ugh, I have to get ready for my date," I mumble to myself.

I notice a missed call from Bella. I tap her name, calling her number and put my phone to my ear. "Merry Christmas, Meredith!" she greets me.

"Merry Christmas, Bella!" I reply.

"Are you getting ready for your date?" she inquires, pure excitement in her voice.

"I'm just about to now," I inform her. "I was Christmas shopping and just finished wrapping all my presents for everyone," I add as explanation. "I'm not sure what I should wear, though," I ponder, as I walk over to my closet.

"Wear your red dress," she insists. "It's perfect for a Christmas Eve date," she proclaims.

I chuckle at the determination in her tone, but I think she's right. "You know what, I think that's a great idea," I agree.

"Fantastic! You go get ready and I'll be over in a little bit to see you before you leave," she enlightens me.

"Okay, thanks," I respond. "I'll leave the front door unlocked for you," I add.

"Okay, bye," she mumbles and disconnects the call.

I set my phone down on my nightstand and reach into my closet, pulling out my red dress. It's a long-sleeved, form fitting dress, falling just above my knees. It has a V-neck, with a one-inch strip of fabric around my neck, connecting to the zipper in the back. I hold it up, looking it over, before I turn and make my way to the bathroom to shower and get ready.

After I get out of the shower, I dry my hair, leaving the long curls to hang mostly down my back. I take a small part of each side and twist it together, connecting them in the back, to pull just enough out of my face. Then I put on my make-up, finishing with a touch of red lipstick. I brush my lips together and take one more glance in the mirror. Then I walk into my room and slip my feet into simple black pumps, before I make my way downstairs.

Bella, already here, turns from her spot on the couch as I descend. Thaddeus is curled up in her lap and she maintains the soothing motion down his back, keeping him content. She's dressed comfortably in dark skinny jeans and an olive green V-neck sweater. "Wow," she murmurs. "You look fantastic," she praises, emphatically.

My heart begins to pound, as I feel my face heat. I look down at my dress as I stop in front of her. "You really think so?" I prompt, anxiously.

"Absolutely!" she confirms.

"Not too over the top?" I prod.

She shakes her head in response. "No. You look amazing," she reiterates, smiling at me in encouragement.

"Thank you," I murmur, with a smile on my face. I look down at Bella and my smile drops at the realization that I'm not going to be with her for Christmas tomorrow for the first time in a long time. I take a deep breath as it finally hits me full force. "I'm sorry I'm skipping out on Christmas tomorrow," I begin, regretfully.

"Don't sweat it," she insists, waving me off, like it's no big deal.

"I feel awful," I admit. "I'm not spending Christmas with you and your family for the first time in sixteen years," I emphasize.

"It's okay, Mer. Really," she claims, attempting to console me and demonstrating one of the reasons I love her so much.

"I will come over as soon as they start eating dessert," I offer. "Okay?" I prompt.

"Fine," she concedes. She throws her hands up as if exasperated with me. "It will all work out, Meredith," she insists. "Stop being such a worry wart," she teases.

I smile and nod my head in agreement. "Yeah, you're right," I concede.

"Come on," she encourages, "I'll walk you out."

Thaddeus climbs off her lap and she stands up. I reach for my coat and slip it on, while she does the same. Then, I grab my black clutch I put my wallet and keys into and open it, dropping my lipstick and phone inside as well. I snap it closed and turn towards the door with Bella right in front of me. "Bye, Thaddeus," I call as we both step outside. I lock the door and pull it closed behind me. I spin on my heel and we walk out to our cars together.

"Have fun," she prompts, smiling wide in encouragement.

"I hope so," I mumble, nervously. I glance at her and appreciatively murmur, "Thanks for coming by, Bella."

She smiles and waves as she slips into her white Jeep. I wave back as I turn towards my car, anxious to get to the restaurant and see Chris.

Chris

I pull into the parking lot at the small airport, just outside of town. There are a lot of open spots and I'm able to park my car right near the opening of the tall fence, leading inside to the terminal. I turn my car off and step out, closing the door behind me to wait for Meredith's mom and dad. I glance down at my pale blue dress shirt and tan pants, accented with a dark brown leather belt and dress shoes. I smooth my shirt down for I think the tenth time, anxious to meet Meredith's parents. I watch as a classy looking, couple, appearing to be around the same age as my parents, walks out of the three-story, tan, brick building. I hold up the small, white sign with, "BLOCK" written on it in thick black lettering. They both turn towards me with a friendly smile. Her dad is just over six feet tall, with a lean build, a diamond shaped face, thick, gray hair, and blue eyes. He's wearing olive green dress pants and dark brown shoes, with a white button up shirt and navy blue V-neck sweater peaking out from underneath a black, wool pea coat. Her mom is about five feet nine inches, with a slim build, brown hair, just like her daughter's, pulled back into a low, ponytail, twisted at the base and blue eyes. The bottom of her black dress, hangs out from underneath her black fur coat.

"Chris Ackerman?" Karl inquires, as they approach.

I paste a smile on my face and announce, "That's me." I drop the sign to my side and hold my hand out to him in greeting. He reaches towards me, meeting me halfway and clasping my hand in a firm grasp. "Nice to meet you, Dr. Block," I proclaim, as we shake hands.

"Karl, please," he insists. He drops my hand and turns towards the beautiful woman standing next to him. He gestures to her and introduces her with clear pride in his voice. "This is my wife, Karen."

I reach my hand out to her and smile as we shake hands. "Nice to meet you," I repeat.

"It's a pleasure," she declares. "Thank you for flying us up for dinner. That's very generous of you," she acknowledges.

My smile broadens, feeling both excited and nervous for Meredith's reaction. "Meredith is going to be very surprised," I assert.

They glance at each other and share a smile of their own, before they return their focus to me. "It's been a long time since we spent Christmas Eve with her," Karen admits.

"We haven't seen her in a quite a while, either," Karl adds, regretfully.

I can't stop my grimace, but I press my lips tightly together, attempting to pull myself together. "So I've heard," I grumble. I clear my throat and force a smile. "Shall we?" I suggest, gesturing to my car.

They both nod and smile politely in acknowledgment. I open the back door for Karen and she folds herself inside. I close the door behind her, as Karl walks around to the other side of the car. I slip in behind the wheel, as Karl climbs in next to me. We buckle our seatbelts and I start my car and back out of the parking spot. I pull out of the gates at the airport and onto the road. "It will only take us about ten minutes to get to the restaurant," I inform them.

"Great," Karen declares. "Thank you, again," she reiterates.

"I'm happy to do it," I reveal, honestly. "Meredith has been working really hard to get everything ready for my family and me for Christmas. She deserves something special for herself. Plus, I know how much she wants to see you, especially for Christmas," I emphasize. It's hard to decide what to tell them. I don't want to speak for Meredith, but after everything she's told me, I think they should know how hard it is on her to not be with them for the holidays. I want to be there for her, without crossing any lines, but honestly, I'd do anything for her.

I glance over and notice a pensive look on Karl's face. He takes a deep breath and glances at me. "So, Chris, exactly what is it you do?" he questions.

"I'm the head of Sales and Marketing for a big toy and baby supply company based out of New York City," I inform them, keeping it simple. I'm not about to tell them I just quit my job when I'm meeting them for the first time.

"That must keep you busy," Karen acknowledges.

I nod my head in agreement, "Normally, but I'm taking some time off to spend time with my family for the holidays."

We pull into the parking lot at the Italian restaurant, all decorated for Christmas. Their name, Casa Di Fratelli is written in a bold, black script on the front of the building. The outside of the brick building has white lights outlining the roof and sides of the building and surrounding every window and door. In every front window, a sparkling snowflake about one and a half feet in diameter, hangs from the top of the sill, shimmering in the lights. The burgundy, green and white awning comes out about ten feet at the entrance and is also strung with white lights. Thick, green garland wraps around the white poles and borders the dark red front door, accented with a large, green wreath decorated with round gold and silver ornaments and a cranberry bow. "Here we are," I broadcast, as I pull to a stop and put the car in park.

"This looks beautiful," Karen murmurs. We all unbuckle and climb out of the car, walking towards the restaurant.

My heart begins to pound in anticipation as we approach the door. I pull the door open and allow her mom and dad to walk in before me. I step inside and barely hold back a gasp at the sight of Meredith with her back to me. She looks stunning in a red dress as she hands her coat over the podium to the blonde coat check girl in a black dress. The maître-d stops us, pulling my attention to him. He's dressed in a black suit with a white shirt and red tie. He's about five feet seven inches with a lean build, a strong jaw and a dimple on his chin. He has dark brown hair and matching brown eyes. "Merry Christmas!" he proclaims, greeting us with a wide smile. "Reservation?" he inquires.

I nod my head in confirmation. "Yes, Ackerman," I announce, keeping my gaze on Meredith. I don't want to take a chance of missing her reaction.

"Ah, yes. Right here," he confirms. "However, I see the reservation is only for three," he proclaims.

I nod in agreement, "That's correct."

His eyebrows draw down in confusion. "A young woman just checked on this reservation. Wouldn't you be four?" he prompts.

I shake my head and reveal, "No, I won't be dining with them."

"What?" Karl questions, arching his eyebrows in surprise.

"Why not?" Karen probes, bringing my attention to both of them.

"Oh, I don't want to impose," I begin. This was about doing something for Merry and her family. It's not about me.

"Absolutely not. I insist you join us," she offers, emphatically.

Meredith straightens at the sound of her mom's voice and slowly turns around, with her mouth hanging open. The moment she spots her parents, she gasps, while her eyes widen further in shock. She shakes her head slightly, as if what she's seeing can't possibly be real. I gulp down the lump in my throat, feeling overwhelmed with emotion as I watch their interaction. I absolutely made the right decision bringing them here. I'd do more for her if I could. I just want her to be happy. She deserves it. She deserves everything.

Chapter 22

Meredith

I step inside the restaurant and look around. It's an Italian restaurant and I believe the décor represents the food wonderfully. The walls are a pale yellow with a white chair rail and moldings and a soft beige underneath. They walls are decorated with wine bottles from Italy, grapes and colorful pictures that make you feel as if you are in Italy itself. The tables are covered with a tan tablecloth and then a white tablecloth over the top. Each chair in the dining area is covered with a simple tan chair cover, bringing the whole room together. Towards the back is a bar area with an elegant dark mahogany bar, with matching stools lined along the front and small tables for two pushed up against the wall. The whole restaurant is decorated for Christmas, increasing its appeal even more. Red velvet bows, red reindeer or red and white Santa wall decorations are hung tastefully on the walls, all around the restaurant. The large picture windows each have a large snowflake, accented by the outside lights on the top and a beautiful white vase with red roses sitting on the sill in the bottom.

"Merry Christmas!" the Maître-D says, welcoming me. I turn to him with a smile, admiring the beautiful seven and a half foot Christmas tree behind him, decorated with white lights, silver, gold and blue round ornaments, silver star ornaments, small red velvet bows and topped with a star, with white lights. The bottom has a simple ivory and silver tree skirt. "Reservation?" he questions, politely.

I nod my head and confirm, "Yes. I'm meeting someone here, I inform him. "Ackerman," I declare.

He pulls up the clipboard, I didn't realize he was holding and skims through his list. "Oh, they have not yet arrived," he enlightens me. He looks at me and suggests, "Would you like to check your coat?"

I nod my head and mumble, "Sure."

"The coat check is over there," he advises, pointing to the large oak desk just beyond the Christmas tree.

"Thank you," I acknowledge and step up to the woman behind the desk. I hold my coat out to her and she takes it with a broad smile. She hangs my coat over a hanger and tears off the bottom half of the ticket from around the hook and hands it to me in return. "Thank you," I repeat, this time to her. Then she turns and makes her way to the large closet behind her with my coat in hand.

I straighten at the sound of a woman who sounds exactly like my mother, but that can't be. I have to be hearing things. I turn around and my mouth drops slightly open at the sight of Chris standing next to my mom and dad. I gasp in shock, while my eyes go as wide as saucers. I shake my head as if I'm seeing things. "Mom? Dad?" I question, with complete disbelief.

"Surprise!" Chris announces, with a smile meant for me.

My heart lodges itself in my throat as I look at him with complete awe. He knew about this? I gulp, fighting back the tears that want to break through. I step towards my mom and throw my arms around her and then I do the same with my dad, reveling in the feeling as their arms wrap around me in return and squeeze me tight. I take a step back from them and look back and forth between them. I open my mouth, finally able to speak and question, "What are you doing here?"

"Merry Christmas, Meredith!" my mom proclaims. She smiles brightly as she looks at me.

"But you hate surprises," I challenge, not able to wipe the smile from my face.

"Yes, but you love them, don't you?" my dad prompts.

"I do," I croon, happily.

I hug my dad again, not able to believe they're standing in front of me. "Merry Christmas, Honey," he whispers in my ear.

"I can't believe you're here," I murmur, echoing my thoughts.

I take a step back to look at them again. "It was all Chris's idea," my dad declares.

I have a quick intake of breath, as I turn to look at Chris, suddenly overwhelmed with my feelings for him. I smile at him and he returns my smile. The depth of the warmth in his look goes straight to my heart. "Thank you," I mumble, attempting to put how grateful I am into two simple words, but that's impossible. I step towards him and wrap my arms around him, hugging him tightly in appreciation. His hands fall to my back, as he accepts my gesture. I reluctantly release him and step back. I look up at him, with my heart full and I want to say so much more.

"Well," he begins, as he drops his hands awkwardly to his sides. "I'll leave you three to dinner, then," he proclaims.

"What?" I ask, confused. "No!" I refuse. "You have to join us," I request, emphatically. After everything he did to make this happen, I want him right here by my side.

"That's what we said," my mom agrees.

"Are you sure?" Chris prods, hesitantly.

"Absolutely. Yes," I confirm, leaving no room for argument.

"We insist, Chris," my dad declares in support.

Chris glances up at the maître-D and questions, "Can you add a fourth person?"

He nods his head and smiles, "Yes, of course. It's no problem at all."

"Thank you," he murmurs in appreciation.

I hug my parents again, completely overjoyed that they're here to have dinner with me for Christmas Eve. I'm smiling so wide, my cheeks are already beginning to hurt. We are shown to our table and Chris pulls my chair out for me, before sitting down next to me. My dad sits on my other side, while my mom sits down across from me.

We order and eat an incredibly delicious dinner while catching up with one another and sharing our plans for tomorrow. I'm thrilled they're getting the chance to get to know Chris after I've spent so much time with him this month. We've gotten close and he really has come to mean a lot to me. My stomach twists suddenly at the realization that our time might be coming to an end. Chris doesn't have to see me after Christmas. I thought tonight was a date, but now that I know it's not. I give myself a mental shake and bring my focus back to my mom and dad as we finish our dessert. "Thank you so much for coming tonight," I repeat. They both smile in response.

"It's too bad you can't stay for dinner tomorrow," Chris acknowledges.

"If I had known how much it meant to Meredith, we would have been here," my mom claims.

I flinch, just a little bit, wondering if that could be true. "Maybe next year," my dad comments.

"Yeah, maybe," I mumble, feeling my excitement begin to deflate.

"Meredith, Honey, you really need to communicate with us better," my mom declares.

My eyebrows draw down in confusion. "What do you mean?" I ask, needing clarification.

"I never knew how important the holidays were to you," she claims, causing my stomach to flip with guilt. I look at her with a questioning gaze.

"Neither did I," my dad adds, bringing my attention to him. "We just thought that you wanted to spend the holidays with Isabella because she had a bigger family than we did," he enlightens me.

I gasp in shock. "What? No! Never!" I blurt out.

"We didn't want you to feel like you had to spend the holidays with us. We just wanted you to have fun," my mom explains.

"We wanted you to enjoy the holidays," he adds for emphasis.

I shake my head in near disbelief, trying to comprehend everything they're telling me. "I always enjoyed spending time with you, Daddy," I insist. "I thought you didn't want to be around me." I attempt to gulp down the lump in my throat and then a little quieter, I reveal, "I thought you didn't want me."

Both my parents look at me with wide eyes, shocked by my admission. "Didn't want you?" my dad reiterates, the words a sour taste in his mouth. "Don't be absurd! We love you," he declares, passionately.

"But, all those years of me decorating alone," I prod, shaking my head, still puzzled.

"We thought you wanted it that way," he claims. "We didn't want to bother you."

"You never asked!" I exclaim, a little defensive.

"Meredith," my mom begins, delicately, "neither did you. We just thought..." she trails off and looks to my dad for help.

"We thought you were ashamed of us," he finishes.

I gasp, my heart clenching painfully at our complete misunderstandings, one after another. I would never feel that way about my parents. "Ashamed of you?" I repeat, my voice cracking with emotion. "Why?" I ask, perplexed.

"You never brought any friends to the house," my mom reminds me.

"I didn't want to bother you while you were working," I explain.

"You never invited us to visit you during college," my mom adds.

"I thought you were too busy," I reiterate.

Chris interrupts, leaning towards me, almost protectively. "If you don't mind me stepping in here, I think a good New Year's Resolution for all of you would be to open up to one another more," he voices.

I glance at him and smile appreciatively. "Agreed," my dad concurs.

I turn to both of my parents and smile, "Definitely."

I watch as my dad lifts his glass and holds it out to me and then to the rest of the table. I reach for my glass, as my mom and Chris follow suit. "To new beginnings," my dad announces.

We all reach towards the middle and tap our glasses gently. I smile, listening to them clink together. Then, I repeat the sentiment, "To new beginnings." I take a sip of the champagne and set my glass down on the table.

A few minutes later, we reluctantly make our way to the coat check, knowing my mom and dad have to make their return flight home. Chris helps me slip my coat on, briefly resting his hands on my shoulders as he pulls it up. I turn to face him and he looks down at me, his eyes full of concern. "Are you sure you want to drive them to the airport?" he prods. "I don't mind," he reiterates.

I smile in acknowledgement, but insist, "Yes, I'm sure. I want to spend as much time with them as I can before they have to get on the plane."

He nods his head in understanding and concedes, "Okay."

"Thank you for this, Chris. I'll never forget it," I confess, attempting to convey with my eyes and simple words how I'm truly feeling. I wrap my arms around him and squeeze him tightly, not able to hold back. His hands fall to my back as he hugs me back, making me smile. I briefly acknowledge how wonderful I feel in his arms.

He releases me as my mom and dad step up to us, but keeps his arm casually around my waist, keeping me close. "Are you sure you can't stay for dinner tomorrow?" he repeats, trying one more time.

My mom grimaces and shakes her head, her eyes full of regret. "No. I have to work," she reiterates.

"Maybe next year?" my dad proposes, sounding hopeful.

"That would be great," Chris proclaims, making my heart skip a beat. Does that mean he thinks we'll be spending next Christmas together? I take a deep breath, trying to reign in my feelings. He could just mean he wants to hire me again.

"Let's go," I encourage. "You don't want to miss your flight."

My mom turns and hugs Chris. He quickly returns her hug and steps back. "Thank you, Chris. This was really, really special," she emphasizes, appreciatively.

"You're welcome," he replies.

My dad reaches out and shakes Chris's hand. "Anytime you want to come down to Baltimore, you're always welcome," he offers.

Chris laughs softly in response and mumbles, "Thanks."

I look at him one more time, waiting until he meets my gaze with his soft blue eyes. I smile and murmur, "Goodnight, Chris."

"Night," he mumbles. "Drive safe, Meredith."

I smile and walk out the door. Chris follows us and turns towards his car, while I climb in mine with my mom and dad. I look over at them, my dad sitting next to me in the passenger seat and my mom sitting behind him in the back. This moment feels completely surreal, but I'm incredibly happy and it's all thanks to Chris. "I guess we have to go," I mumble. I buckle my seat belt and start my car. Then I back out of the parking lot and pull back out onto Main Street.

"So, Chris seems really nice," my mom, acknowledges. I feel her eyes on me, watching me for my reaction.

I feel my face turn cherry red, but I'm not sure if they notice, with the lights of the gages on the dashboard and the streetlights our only light. "He is," I mumble in agreement, smiling. Tonight was absolutely perfect.

Chapter 23

Chris

I pat down a few stray hairs before I open the door and walk out of the bathroom. I make my way back downstairs and into the kitchen, now that I'm dressed for the day. I'm wearing tan pants, an indigo blue button-up dress shirt, a navy blue blazer and my brown Oxford dress shoes, with a matching brown belt. My family usually dresses up for Christmas and I want to look extra good this year. I stride directly for the coffee pot, having already brewed the coffee earlier when I woke up. I open the cabinet and reach for a red coffee mug and close the door. I pour myself a cup of coffee and inhale the scent, the smell alone beginning to wake me up. I take a sip as I look around the kitchen. Every room in this house looks like Christmas. Meredith has done an amazing job. It's so much like my Grandfather used to do, but there are some special touches that make it unique and still remind me of him. It's incredible.

I hear the front door slowly creak open, before it closes with a quiet click. Then, the soft tapping of shoes, entering the great room follows, bringing a smile to my face. Meredith is here. I walk into the living room, anxious to see her. I love being able to see her every day. I don't want that to end, but I don't have any idea what she wants or how she feels about me. I find her looking at all the presents underneath the Christmas tree, temporarily pushing my concerns away. As always, she looks incredibly beautiful. She's wearing a fuzzy, cherry red sweater, a slim fitting black skirt that falls just below her knees and short, black velvet ankle boots with a one-inch heel. She has her hair completely down today, the soft brown curls falling delicately over her shoulders. I grin broadly as I watch her. "If you're looking for your present, it's not under there," I tease.

She jumps, her whole body stiffening at the sound of my voice. She looks at me with wide eyes and her hand on her chest, right over her heart. "Oh," she gasps. "Chris. You scared me," she mumbles, breathlessly. I chuckle softly at her reaction. She takes a deep breath and exhales slowly, attempting to pull herself together. Then she drops her hand to her side and smiles, as if starting over. "Good morning," she states.

"Morning," I repeat, grinning down at her. "Merry Christmas," I add. My stomach flip-flops the moment I utter the words to her. I like being able to see her first thing in the morning, especially knowing it's Christmas morning.

"Merry Christmas," she replies, returning my smile.

I take a deep breath to calm myself down before I speak again. "What are you doing?" I inquire, curiously, nodding towards the presents.

"Nothing!" she declares, emphatically. She shakes her head as if in denial, of what I'm not quite sure. Her cheeks turn a beautiful shade of pink, contradicting her response even further. "Just making sure everything is perfect in here," she offers as an excuse.

"It is," I verify, confidently. I pause and narrow my eyes, attempting to figure out what she really was doing, but it is Christmas. I'm not going to push it. She'll tell me when she's ready. I take a deep breath and hold up the mug in my hand. "I made coffee. Would you like some?" I offer.

She breathes a sigh of relief, with my change of subject. Then, she gratefully accepts, "Sure." She follows me into the kitchen. I sit down at the counter, while she walks over to the coffee pot and reaches for a white coffee mug, decorated with green Christmas trees. She pours herself a cup of coffee. Then she walks to the refrigerator and pulls out the cream, adding a splash to her mug, before returning it where she found it. Then she walks over, opposite me and leans her hip against the counter as she takes a sip of her coffee. She meets my gaze and questions, "So, when do you expect people to arrive today?"

"My parents should be here around one," I inform her.

She nods her head in acknowledgement. "Okay," she murmurs, momentarily lost in thought. "Everyone else will be here around three?" she prompts, for clarification. She looks up at me from underneath her long lashes, biting her bottom lip, as she awaits my response.

I nod slowly in confirmation. "That's what I told them," I murmur.

"Great," she mumbles and exhales heavily. She looks around the kitchen anxiously, her eyes going from one side of the room to another.

"Are you okay?" I inquire, my voice full of concern. I tilt my head to the side, assessing her. "You seem nervous," I recognize.

She grimaces and nods her head in affirmation. "Yeah, I am nervous," she concedes, as a small sigh escapes through her lips. She sets her coffee cup on the counter and leans down on her elbows, looking across the counter at me.

My eyebrows draw down in confusion. "Why?" I probe.

"I don't know," she grumbles, seeming irritated with her reaction. "I...I just...I just want everything to be absolutely perfect," she stammers.

I smile reassuringly at her. "It will be, Merry," I proclaim.

She scrunches up her nose adorably. "I hope so," she mumbles.

I set my cup down and stand up, leaning towards her across the counter and wait until she meets my eyes. "Come on," I encourage. "You're a professional. Isn't this just another event you planned," I prompt, in attempt to make her feel better.

She winces at my description and shakes her head in response. "No. I wouldn't call it that," she admits. She glances down at her hands, fidgeting on the counter, before looking anxiously back at me, her cheeks turning a darker shade of red by the second.

"Why not?" I question, desperately needing to hear her explanation. I gulp down the sudden lump in my throat, not wanting to get my hopes up.

"It just," she begins and trails off. She pauses and takes a deep breath, before exhaling slowly. Then she lifts her head and puts her focus completely on me with a renewed determination in her eyes. "It means a lot to me," she states.

"Why?" I push.

She looks into my eyes, her own brown eyes turning soft and tender. "Because you mean a lot to me," she confesses.

My heart lurches and then beats rapidly. Those words uttered from her mouth are exactly what I want to hear. I slowly lean towards her, over the counter, glancing down at her soft lips, letting her know my intention and then returning my gaze to her eyes as I start to close the distance between us. My fingers itch to take her face in my hands as she leans towards me and tilts her head up to me. I move closer to her, until I'm barely an inch away. My own lips begin to tingle in anticipation, as I feel her warm breath on my face. My eyes begin to close, when we're barely a breath apart. Suddenly the doorbell rings, startling us both to opposite sides of the counter. I drop my head in disappointment and heave a regretful sigh. I push away from the counter and grumble, "I'll get it."

She nods stiffly and picks up her coffee cup, taking sip as I walk out of the kitchen. I take a deep breath and exhale slowly, trying to pull myself together, before I open the door. I grasp the handle and pull the door open. My eyes instantly widen in surprise at the sight of my mom and dad standing on the front porch with wide smiles on their faces.

My dad is about two inches taller than my mom, but still shorter than me. I'm told I get my height from my Grandfather. My dad has blue eyes and his brown hair is slightly darker now, peppered with gray and receding slightly. He's wearing tan pants and brown Oxford's like me, but he has a pale blue button down with a little darker blue V-neck sweater pulled over the top. My mom is dressed in a long blush pink skirt, a matching pink silk, V-neck shirt with small black polka dots, and a black sweater cardigan over the top, adorned with diamond-like crystals. Both of them have their black winter coats unzipped and ready to remove. "Christian!" my mom, declares gleefully. She steps inside, immediately setting bags full of gifts down. She opens her arms wide and wraps them around me, hugging me tightly.

"Mom! Dad! Hi," I stammer. I return my mom's hug, both happy to see them and disappointed they're already here. I would've loved more time alone with Merry.

My dad closes the door behind him and hands me a tray of food when my mom releases me. "Merry Christmas, Son," he announces.

"You guys are early," I state the obvious.

"We made great time," my dad proclaims.

"I couldn't wait to get here," my mom admits, without remorse. "Honey," she croons, "the house looks amazing!"

I smile and nod my head in agreement as we glance around the immediate area. "Yeah, wait until you see the rest of the house," I praise. "Meredith did a really great job," I proclaim.

"When do we get to meet her?" my dad inquires.

"She's in the kitchen," I answer, without thinking.

"Great!" my mom exclaims. She slips off her coat and hands it to me, before she immediately begins striding for the kitchen.

"Mom, wait!" I call after her, my arms now full. My dad hands me his coat and follows after her. I toss both of their coats over the banister, planning on hanging them up after they meet Meredith. Then I turn and chase after them, my stomach suddenly twisting with anxiety.

"You must be Meredith," my mom announces, the moment she spots her as she strides determinedly into the kitchen.

Meredith sets her coffee cup down and turns, facing my mom with a wide smile. "I am. Hi. You are?" she questions.

My mom holds her arms out and wraps Meredith in a hug, taking her by surprise. I feel my face heat and my heart start to race. I hope my mom doesn't push her away. "Renee," she informs her, still hugging her. "Chris's mom," she clarifies. Meredith awkwardly hugs her back, patting her gently. "I'm so glad to finally meet you," my mom proclaims, enthusiastically.

201

"Mom, come on," I plead, nervously.

She finally releases Meredith and takes a step back. "What?" she asks, innocently. "I can't hug the woman responsible for all of this?" she prompts, gesturing around the house.

"Oh, I'm just doing my job. It's no big deal," she mumbles, oblivious to my lie. My heart drops to my stomach, knowing I have no right to argue the truth.

My mom takes another step back, her mouth open and her eyes wide with disbelief. "Your job?" she repeats, her disapproval practically echoing in my ears. She spins on her heel and looks up at me, with utter displeasure, more than apparent. "Chris, I told you not to hire anybody," she reiterates, emphatically.

I open my mouth to explain, but Meredith interrupts me before I'm able to say a word. "Oh, that's not what I meant," she claims. "I just meant it's my job because I love Christmas so much," she amends. "You know?" she prods. My heart feels full as I stare at her. She has to understand what I insinuated. I'm incredibly grateful she just covered for me, but does she understand I wish there was truth to my lie. "I feel like it's my responsibility to make sure Chris and his whole family have the best Christmas ever," she adds. She glances in my direction and offers me a secretive smile.

My mom wraps her arms around Meredith again, already looking at her with so much love. I know how she feels. My chest aches with how much I'm feeling for her. How do I feel this much this fast? I don't want to let her go. My mom steps back, still grasping Meredith's arms. "That is so sweet," she proclaims. "I'm so glad Chris found someone like you," she grins.

"Mom," I argue, wanting her to stop. I'm embarrassed for reasons I can't explain aloud, without giving myself away, but I wouldn't change a thing. If I did,

I don't know if I ever would have met Meredith or gotten to know her the way I have. I'm incredibly grateful for all the time I've been able to spend with her. If I had to do it all over again, I'd hire her again in a heartbeat, just to have her close. I already can't imagine not having her in my life. Oddly, I've never been more grateful I didn't listen to my mother.

"What?" she prods, innocently.

My dad steps forward and introduces himself, breaking up the tension. "Hi, Meredith. I'm Chris's dad, Jeff," he states, kindly.

"Please, call me Merry," she requests.

"Here," he offers, taking the pan back from me and handing it to Meredith. "Renee made cornbread," he announces.

"Great," she replies. "Thank you." She turns around and sets the cornbread down on the back counter, along with other already prepared food.

"Let me help you bring your bags in and put the presents underneath the tree," I suggest, looking at my dad. He nods in acknowledgment. "Mom, go check out what Merry did with the great room," I suggest.

"Oh, I can't wait!" she exclaims.

I watch as both of my parents turn and walk towards the front of the house and into the great room. Then I turn to Merry and look into her eyes, wanting to say so much, but not really knowing how to begin. I reach for her hand and give it a gentle squeeze, sending goosebumps up my own arms. "Thanks," I rasp, my voice catching. She smiles up at me, sending my heart racing. More than anything, I want to pull her into my arms and kiss her, shutting out the rest of the world.

"Chris?" my dad calls from the great room. "Are you coming?" he probes.

I exhale slowly and give Meredith's hand a small squeeze. Then, I force myself to let go of her hand and follow my mom and dad into the other room. I glance back at her and smile, watching as Merry turns back to her coffee.

Chapter 24

Meredith

I move around the kitchen, preparing snacks and appetizers and trying to push thoughts of Chris out of my head, but that's utterly impossible when I'm in his house spending Christmas with him and his family. What exactly did he tell his mom about me? Does she think I'm his girlfriend? Butterflies take flight in my stomach at the thought. Does he really feel that way about me? I wish we had a little more time before they arrived today, maybe then he would have finally kissed me. What am I saying? I've been telling myself I can't go there because he's a client, but is that really what I want? Even I'm not stubborn enough to deny how much I like him at this point. I'd be crazy not to, but he's leaving right? He has to go back to New York. I know he has the house here, so it wouldn't be impossible to see each other, but I don't want a relationship where I only get to see him for holidays and vacations. I grimace and remind myself I have no idea how he really feels about me, so specifics on how we could make a relationship work don't really matter unless I get the courage to talk to him about it.

I pick up a large white platter of cheese and crackers in one hand and a red and white platter with chips and salsa in my other hand. Then, I carefully make my way to the game room. I want to keep the simple snacks in there from everything that Chris shared with me. I set them both down on the coffee table, out of the way of the stack of board games and cards sitting in the middle. I stand and spin around to get more snacks to bring in, when Renee steps into the room. "The house really looks marvelous, Merry," she compliments, looking around the room. "I can't believe how much it reminds me of how my dad used to decorate it," she claims, making me smile.

"I'm glad," I admit. "Chris showed me pictures and I really did my best to replicate them as much as possible."

She nods in understanding and mumbles, "Ah." She focuses on me and offers me a sweet smile. "You did a great job," she praises.

I blush and smile appreciatively in response. "Thank you," I murmur.

She takes a step closer to me, her gaze curious. She lowers herself onto the couch and pats the empty spot next to her. "Sit for minute," she requests. I smile and sit down next to her, hoping I'm ready for her interrogation. I try to get comfortable, before I lift my gaze to hers. "So, how long have you known Chris?" she inquires.

"About a month, now" I answer, honestly. "I met him right when he got here," I enlighten her, anxious for what she may ask next. I wish I would have had the chance to talk to Chris about this first.

She arches her eyebrows in surprise. "You're from Christmas Cove?" she prods.

"No," I reply, shaking my head. "I live in South Bristol," I inform her.

"Oh?" she prompts, seeming a little more confused. "How did you meet?" she questions, perplexed.

I smile to myself, thinking about the first morning I met him. "Through his assistant, Beth," I respond, sticking to the truth.

"Blind date?" she probes.

I laugh. I can't help it. She's very persistent. I nod my head and shrug my shoulders, conceding, "You could say that." It may not have been a date, but it was the same idea, sort of.

She stares at me, momentarily assessing me, as if trying to figure me out, while I attempt not to fidget under her scrutiny. "Well," she begins, "he seems really happy," she finally reveals, as she breaks out in a broad smile.

My heartbeat speeds up and heat rushes to my cheeks. I look at her, instantly filled with hope. "You think so?" I prod.

She smiles in encouragement and nods her head in confirmation. "Yes," she murmurs. Her demeanor changes as she continues. "He hasn't been himself since his grandfather passed away almost two months ago," she concedes. She tries to hide her own flinch at her admission.

My heart aches, knowing Chris has had a hard time processing all of it, but I don't blame him. It's not easy to lose someone you love. I nod my head in acknowledgement. "I know they were very close," I recognize.

She grimaces and nods her head in agreement. She confirms, "They were." She pauses and takes a deep breath before she continues. "My dad always wanted to see Chris in a relationship during the holidays, but he never brought a girl here," she confesses.

My eyes widen in surprise. "Really?" I prompt.

"Really," she affirms, nodding her head. "She smiles at me and reveals, "You must be very special, Meredith."

I blush and look down at my lap, as my stomach flip-flops. The doorbell rings and before I have a chance to move, I hear Chris call, "I got it!"

I take a deep breath as I listen to Chris's footsteps cross the foyer. I exhale slowly and look up at Renee and smile. "Well, Chris is very special to me," I enlighten her, my stomach twisting into knots with my confession.

She returns my smile, looking both relieved and thrilled. She leans towards me and simply proclaims, "I'm glad."

"Mom," Chris yells, "the Steins are here," he broadcasts.

"I've talked to Artie several times, but this will be the first time I'm actually meeting him," she informs me. "Do you know Artie Stein?" she inquires.

I nod my head and confirm, "I do. I know his wife, Elaine and his daughter, Shira as well," I apprise her.

"Really?" she asks, obviously surprised.

I nod in confirmation. "Yes, Shira just made her Bat Mitzvah," I enlighten her. "They're a really nice family."

"Mom!" Chris calls, again.

"Okay," she laughs. "I guess we gotta' go, but we'll talk more later," she states. I smile and nod my head in agreement. We both stand up and I follow her up the stairs and into the foyer to greet the Steins.

We step into the foyer together to find Chris and his dad standing with Artie and his family, all dressed up. Artie is wearing a black suit, a pale pink button down dress shirt, a red tie with tiny white polka dots and a long, charcoal wool dress coat with a red scarf hanging around his neck. His wife Elaine is a beautiful women with blonde hair, cut just above her shoulders and a few wisps of bangs, bright blue eyes and a lean build. She's wearing a slimming, sleeveless black dress, accented with golden flowers printed in the fabric, black heels with a slim strap at her ankle and matching black nylons. Their daughter, Shira has the same blue eyes and blonde hair as her mom, but her hair hangs well past her shoulders and she has it styled in loose curls. She's wearing a thin cream sweater with a rose, corduroy dress over the top, adorned with brown buttons down the middle, right in the front of the dress, with her black dress coat hanging open. Her short black leather ankle boots and matching black nylons add to her youthful flair.

The moment we step into the room, Shira's face lights up, with her bright, beautiful smile. "Hi, Merry," she greets me, cheerfully.

"Hi, Shira!" I grin back at her and hold out my arms, as I take a step towards her. "Give me a hug," I request.

She meets me halfway and wraps her arms around and squeezes me tightly, as I do the same. I take a step back and turn towards Elaine.

"It's so wonderful to see you, Merry," Elaine proclaims.

"Thank you. You too, Elaine," I respond. I turn towards Artie, maintaining my smile. "Hi, Artie," I state.

"Hello, Merry. Merry Christmas," Artie adds. I nod and smile at him in appreciation, knowing they don't celebrate Christmas.

Chris steps in. "Elaine, Artie, Shira, meet my mother, Renee Ackerman," he announces, holding his hand out towards his mom. "Mom, this is the Stein family," he proclaims, gesturing to the three of them.

Renee steps up to Artie and hugs him, taking him by surprise. "Artie," she murmurs and then takes a step back. "It is so nice to finally meet you in person, Artie," she emphasizes.

"Likewise," he agrees. "I'm so sorry about your dad," he grimaces, offering his condolences. "He was a great man," he adds, solemnly.

Renee forces a small smile and murmurs, "Thank you. We certainly miss him," she acknowledges.

Shira turns to me and questions, "What are you doing here, Merry?"

"Oh, celebrating Christmas, of course," I proclaim.

"She's being humble," Renee comments, mischievously. She glances at the Steins and grins proudly. "She's dating my son," she whispers.

Chris's cheeks instantly turn red and I'm sure my own cheeks come close to matching. "Mom!" he cautions.

Elaine turns to me, with wide eyes. "Is that so?" she prompts, curiously. "I'm so glad. You're such a lovely young woman, Merry. It's about time you found a nice man," she declares.

I open my mouth to respond, feeling my face heat even more, but I quickly snap it closed, not able to say anything.

"Mom!" Shira pleads, desperately. She stares hard at her mom through narrowed eyes, giving her a warning glare.

"Elaine, come on now. It's none of your business," Artie emphasizes. The corners of his mouth twitch up in amusement, as he fights a smile.

"You can say that again," Shira grumbles, irritably.

"What?" Elaine asks, innocently. "I was going to introduce her to your cousin Joshua at Shira's Bat Mitzvah, but I ran out of time," she claims.

I smile as I feel my face heat even more. "Mom!" Shira scolds and I can't help but be grateful. "You're embarrassing her and me," she complains, gesturing in my direction.

Chris steps forward and thankfully successfully changes the subject as he offers, "Why don't I take your coats upstairs?" They all begin slipping off their coats and handing them over to Chris.

"I can take the wine," I state. I hold out my hands and take the bottle of wine from Elaine, smiling politely. "Thank you," I repeat, as she hands me the bottle.

I turn around and walk back into the kitchen, my nerves going a little haywire inside my stomach. I'm not really sure how to take everything and I can't wait to have some time to talk to Chris after this is all over. I set the wine down next to a few other bottles I already pulled out for today. Then, I turn around and continue working on putting out all the appetizers and snacks, while we wait for everyone else to arrive.

I walk back into the kitchen, ready to move on to my next task and begin making room for the dinner. The doorbell rings and again Chris calls, "I'll get it." A moment later, he yells for me, "Meredith, will you come in here a minute?" he requests.

"Coming," I reply and change directions, walking towards the foyer. I step into the room with a wide smile; curious as to whom I'm about to meet.

"Surprise!" Bella and her whole family announce in unison, along with Chris.

I gasp as my mouth drops open in shock. "Oh, my gosh!" I exclaim. "What are all of you doing here?" I question.

Bella grins and informs me, "Chris invited us." I look at Chris, my heart feeling like it's about to burst, as he smiles at me. He gives me a small shrug of his shoulders, like this was no big deal, but this is everything to me. They have always been my second family and treated me like one of their own for the holidays. I hold my breath, fighting back my tears. "Merry Christmas," Bella declares, pulling her attention back to me. She steps up to me and wraps her arms around me, giving me a hug.

I hug her back and exhale slowly. I release her and take a step back. "You look beautiful," I compliment.

She's wearing a gorgeous deep cranberry, sleeveless, velvet jumpsuit, with a deep V in the front and black heels with a thick strap around her ankle and pointed toes. She pulls off her orange winter coat and folds it over her arm.

"Thank you," she replies.

Bella turns and takes a tray of food from her mom. Then her mom instantly puts her arms out and steps towards me, wrapping me up in her arms. Bella looks just like her mom, although she's about an inch shorter than Bella. Her whole family has the same brown eyes and dark brown hair, just cut and styled differently. Her mom's hair hangs straight just past her shoulders. She's wearing a simple black dress with a cream cardigan over the top. "Merry Christmas, Merry," she proclaims, as she releases me.

Bella's baby sister, Jessica, smiles brightly and gives me a quick hug, wishing me a "Merry Christmas." She's not exactly a baby anymore, but she is still a teenager. She slips off her black winter coat, underneath wearing a stylish, long-sleeved, amethyst purple dress with straps from the shoulders connecting at the bottom of a small V with a gold charm. She wears her hair long and straight and she's only an inch or two shorter than Bella now.

"Merry Christmas, Jess," I reply. "You look great," I compliment her.

"Thanks," she responds.

"Merry Christmas," her dad rasps, as I hug him next. He's a tall man at six feet one inch with broad shoulders and a neatly trimmed beard and mustache. He's dressed in a black suit with a white dress shirt and a golden tie, decorated with red and white and green and white buoys, bringing a smile to my face. His familiar tan scarf with stripes of red, black and white hangs around his neck.

Bella's youngest brother, Kevin is about three inches taller than her, with a lean build and his dark hair neatly trimmed. He's wearing black pants with a cranberry crewneck sweater, under his black coat. He grins, repeating, "Merry Christmas."

I give him a quick hug and then hug her other brother, Brian and his wife Lauren. Brian cuts his hair close to his head and he has a faint shadow of a beard and mustache. He's just barely taller than Bella, with broad shoulders. He's dressed nice in black pants and a burgundy button down shirt. His wife Lauren has straight, brown hair, cut just above her shoulders, with pale skin and blue eyes. She's wearing a burgundy dress with a cream and dark green floral print and a matching burgundy cardigan, with black, one-inch heels with three straps around her ankle. She's cradling their new baby in her arms, holding him close to her chest. His big blue eyes look exactly like his mom's. She tugs off his pale blue hat, exposing his tuft of reddish brown hair on top of his head. I help as she peels off his dark blue coat for him, while Brian holds everything else for her and the baby. He turns his head and looks at me, his blue eyes full of curiosity. "He's so big," I murmur, holding out my hand to him. He reaches out and grasps my pointer finger, with his tiny little fingers. I smile wide at him and he giggles in response. He's wearing an adorable red and green plaid shirt and little black corduroy pants. "You're so cute," I croon. He smiles adorably in response.

"I'll take your coats," Chris offers. Everyone begins handing their coats over to him before they turn to walk inside.

I gently tug my finger free and step towards Chris, his arms now full of coats. "Chris," I mumble, wanting to say so much, but not knowing exactly what to say to express my extreme gratitude for this man. He smiles and gives me a knowing look, filling my heart up with pure joy.

"We'll talk later," he mumbles. Then he turns and walks upstairs with the large pile of coats. I spin on my heel and follow after Bella, into the kitchen, overwhelmed with emotion. I take a deep breath and exhale slowly, pushing it aside for now so I'm able to finish preparing dinner.

Chapter 25

Chris

I smile to myself, as I set all the coats down on the bed in one of the spare bedrooms. The look on Meredith's face was exactly what I hoped for. She's so happy, just as she deserves to be. I make my way back downstairs, passing by the great room where I find my parents, Artie and Elaine Stein, as well as Mr. and Mrs. Franz talking and laughing with one another. I walk through the kitchen, spotting Merry and Bella deep in conversation as they set up for dinner. Then I make my way into the game room finding Bella's siblings and sister-in-law, along with Shira, playing with the baby.

The doorbell rings and I spin around, turning right back to the front door. "I got it," I call out. I open the door to find Aunt Jean, Uncle Scott and my cousins Clint, Emma and Elisabeth. "Merry Christmas," I announce in greeting.

They reply almost in unison, "Merry Christmas!"

Aunt Jean is a few inches shorter than me, with a lean build, high cheekbones, brown hair and blue eyes. I give my Aunt Jean a kiss on the cheek. "It's good to see you," I murmur. Aunt Jean slips off her cranberry winter coat to reveal a long-sleeved black dress, with simple black pumps, with a one and a half inch heel and a long silver medallion necklace around her neck.

"We're happy to be here," Uncle Scott proclaims, with a broad smile. I reach my hand out to shake his. He's about the same height as me with broad shoulders and light brown skin. He has short black hair, a little longer on top, brown eyes and black-rimmed glasses. He

215

has a long, dark green winter coat over on, over navy dress pants with a hazy blue button-up shirt, red tie and a cranberry crewneck sweater over the top.

My cousin Clint reaches out and I shake his hand, as we both reach in with our free hands, giving one another a firm pat on the back. He looks so much like his dad, with his light brown skin, a touch lighter than Uncle Scott, dark brown wavy hair, a little longer on top, soft brown eyes and a wide smile like Aunt Jean's. Underneath his black dress coat he's dressed in navy blue and dark green plaid pants with a white button down shirt and a navy blue sweater pulled over the top, accented with his dark brown Oxfords. "Are we going to play some cards later?" I prompt.

He nods his head in affirmation, "Definitely."

My cousin, Emma steps towards me, giving me a one armed hug, as she leans over little sister, Elisabeth. "Merry Christmas, Chris." Emma looks so much like her mom, except she has long blonde hair, with her mom's blue eyes, and more of an oval face like Uncle Scott. She takes off her coat and drapes it over her arm, showing her beautifully patterned navy and white sleeveless dress, accented short, dark brown boots.

She smiles up at me and I reiterate, "Merry Christmas."

I crouch down to my cousin Elisabeth's height. She's only six years old and a perfect mix of her mom and dad. She has long brown hair, big brown eyes, pale skin and a bright smile. She's always wonderful at bringing a smile to everyone's faces. She's wearing a red sleeveless dress, underneath her raspberry pink winter coat, with winter white patent leather shoes. "You look very pretty, Elisabeth," I compliment her.

"Thanks," she grins. "We brought presents," she broadcasts, happily. She holds a red wrapped box out to me, with pure excitement in her eyes.

I chuckle softly and inform her, "I think there might be one or two things under the tree for you too." Her eyes widen and she glances up at her mom and dad, as if asking permission to go inside with her eyes.

"Why don't you give me your coat and you can go take a look," I suggest.

She slips it off and takes off almost instantly and we all laugh in response. "Be careful," Aunt Jean calls after her.

The rest of them hand me their coats and go inside, while I make my way up to the spare room to set their coats down. The doorbell rings on my way back downstairs and I instantly turn to pull the door open, finding Aunt Marie, Uncle Jack and Jack, Jr. on the other side, bundled in their black winter coats. "Merry Christmas," they proclaim.

"Merry Christmas," I reply, as they step inside and I close the door behind them. Aunt Marie is holding a tray of food off to the side as she leans in and gives me a kiss on the cheek. She's the shortest of her siblings. She has auburn red hair and golden brown eyes. She's wearing a black dress with black and silver dress loafers.

Uncle Jack reaches out to shake my hand, smiling wide underneath his gray mustache. He's about the same height as me, with a lean build, brown hair and blue eyes. He's dressed in tan pants, a light blue shirt, with a dark blue striped tie and a navy blue sport coat. "I'm happy you're here," I declare.

I grin at Jack, Jr. and reach out to shake his hand. He pulls me in and we give one another a firm pat on the back. We're the closest in age of all my cousins. He's about two inches shorter than me with a lean build, dark brown hair, brown eyes and a tightly trimmed beard and mustache. He's wearing charcoal dress pants and a white button down shirt, keeping it simple. "It's good to see you, Chris," he proclaims.

"You too, Jack," I acknowledge. I turn back to Aunt Marie and hold my hands out for the tray of food. I offer, "Let me take that for you."

"Thank you," she replies.

"I'll take our coats upstairs and throw them on the bed in the spare room," Jack proposes.

"Thanks, Jack." I reply, appreciatively.

I make my way into the kitchen and set the tray of food down on an open spot at the back of the kitchen counter. "This is from my Aunt Marie," I inform Merry.

"Thanks, Chris," she grins. "Why don't you go catch up with your family," she suggests. "Bella is helping me in here," she apprises me.

"Thanks," I murmur. I smile at her and turn around to go find my cousins.

Jack, Clint, Kevin and myself play a few games of Hearts, while Lauren, Emma, Jessica and Shira talk and laugh, while Brian watches over Elisabeth as she plays with the baby on the floor.

It doesn't feel like long before Meredith calls all of us into the kitchen. "Dinner is ready, everyone," she announces.

We walk into the kitchen and notice Meredith has the turkey situated at the head of the table with a carving knife. My mom steps up to me and puts her hand on my back in support. "It's time for you to take over for Grandpa," she declares, nodding towards the turkey.

I attempt to gulp down the sudden lump in my throat. I nod my head in acceptance and rasp, "Okay." I paste a smile on my face and step up to the chair at the head of the table, feeling a sudden wave of sadness. I take a deep breath and exhale slowly, steadying myself, before I lift my head and look at my family. I let my gaze roam over everyone around the room, until my eyes land on Meredith. She smiles in encouragement and I instantly feel the tension, slowly easing out of me.

I lift the carving knife and fork and slice the first piece of turkey. I lift it up, using the carving fork and carefully set it down on the platter in front of me. Then I look back up at my family and nod in my mother's direction, hoping she'll lead us in prayer. I close my eyes as she begins, letting my mind drift to everything I'm thankful for. I'm grateful for my family, all the time I had with Grandpa, although there's never enough and I miss him every day. I'm grateful for Merry, I admit, my heart clenching at thoughts of her. "Amen," my mom finishes the prayer.

"Amen," we all echo.

"Everyone, grab a plate and find a seat. Meredith is an incredible cook," I compliment. I finish carving the turkey, filling the platter as I go. Then I grab my own plate and make my way around to all of Meredith's food, along with dishes from our other guests. I make sure to find room for a little of everything on my plate, before making my way back to my seat.

I listen to the low rumble of conversation, hearing numerous compliments on both the house and the food. "I have to give Merry all the credit. She's absolutely wonderful," I praise, over and over again. I glance across the room at Meredith and I can't help, but smile. I watch as her head falls back in laughter, while chatting with Bella and Lauren. My heart clenches, sending tingles down my spine at the sight. She's absolutely stunning. I tear my gaze away from her and turn back to Jack and Clint. "I think it's time for dessert," I reveal quietly, hoping to get there before Aunt Minnie's Chocolate Cream Pie is gone.

Jack laughs, "I think we have to cleanup first," he reminds me. I shrug in response. We help clean the kitchen up quickly, switching over to dessert. I cut myself a piece of the chocolate cream pie, along with one of Meredith's cookies. I make my way back to my seat and take a bite, enjoying the sweet, familiar taste. I look across the room, searching for Merry, as I eat my pie. I spot her setting down another tray of cookies on the end of the counter. She turns and I catch her eye, smiling at her in both appreciation and admiration. She's truly an incredible woman.

She blushes a beautiful shade of red and looks down as she makes her way over to me. "How was everything?" she prompts.

"Everything was delicious," I compliment her. "Absolutely perfect," I insist. She nods and smiles in response. "Did you eat enough?" I question. She seemed to be moving around the kitchen more than anything. I want to make sure she takes care of herself.

She nods her head in confirmation. "I did," she states. I arch my eyebrows in challenge and she reiterates, "I ate more than enough." She emphasizes her point with a smirk and a pat on her stomach, making me chuckle. "Do you mind if I say a few words?" she requests, appearing a little nervous.

"Of course," I answer.

She steps up beside my chair and looks down at me, giving me one more look, as if needing the encouragement. I nod my head and smile, hoping I'm able to give her what she needs. "May I have your attention, please?" she requests, loudly.

"Great meal, Merry!" Brian calls, loudly. Everyone cheers in agreement and her cheeks turn a beautiful shade of pink.

"Thank you," she replies. Then she takes a deep breath and straightens her shoulders, before she continues. "I have a little surprise for Chris and his family," she reveals, with a glance in my direction. My eyes widen in surprise. I thought I'd already seen everything. She looks back at everyone and states, "I'm really not one for public speaking, so if everyone can put on their coats and shoes and come outside, I'd love to show you."

I push my chair back and stand up. I look down at her, my eyes full of curiosity. "What is this all about?" I question.

She wiggles her eyebrows and grins mischievously. "You'll see," she declares, only increasing my interest.

I smile at her and mumble, "Guess I better go get my coat then."

It takes about ten minutes, before we're all bundled up and gathered outside. Meredith stands on the steps of the porch, holding a plug in her hand. I step up beside her in support, while the rest of our friends and my family stand on the lawn in front of us, looking up at the house. She glances at me and takes a deep breath, before turning towards everyone else. "Chris told me that his grandpa had a theme when it came to decorating the outside of his house every year. I wanted to stick with doing a theme, but I wanted to do something really special," she emphasizes. She turns to look at me and continues, "Chris, that night when we found out that your grandpa made my Aunt Minnie's chocolate cream pie every year, I knew that he was smiling down on you, on your family, on this house," she pauses. I watch as her

Adam's apple bobs up and down as she gulps. "Maybe even on us," she adds, smiling up at me, causing my heart to skip a beat.

"Awe," I hear my mom croon.

"That night, I knew what the theme was going to be," she declares. "Merry Christmas, everyone," she announces and plugs in the cord.

The whole house lights up, decorated with large angels in both blue and white lights. I've never seen anything so beautiful, both the meaning and the sight. My heart lodges itself in my throat and I momentarily gasp for breath as I hear the sounds of amazement from everyone around me.

"It's angels, Daddy!" I hear Elisabeth's excited declaration.

"It sure is, Honey," Uncle Scott replies.

"Just like Poppi," she reiterates in her sweet voice. "It's like he's here with us," she proclaims.

My heart clenches with so many emotions. I look at Meredith and smile in appreciation, as I hold my breath and fight back tears. My family hugs one another, everyone suddenly emotional. Meredith smiles and I return her smile as best I can, trying to convey how much this means to me without being able to say them aloud quite yet. My eyes roam back to the house, taking it all in. A few minutes later, I look for her again and realize she's missing. I turn and make my way inside the house in search of Meredith, needing to see her.

Chapter 26

Meredith

While everyone strolls around the yard, looking at the outdoor lights and decorations in awe, I sneak back into the house through the sliding glass door by the game room, when I think no one is looking. I make my way upstairs and slip off my coat. I walk over to the front closet and pull the door open. I hang up my coat and close the door. Then I wander into the great room and look up at the Christmas tree. It's really beautiful with the white lights, gold bows, gold pine cones and gorgeous silver and gold angels hanging all over the tree, with a white angel draped over the top of the tree. I'm happy with how all the decorations turned out.

I sigh and wrap my arms tightly around my middle and give myself a squeeze. I'm feeling a little emotional today, especially when I think about everything that has happened recently. I've really enjoyed having dinner with Chris every night for nearly a month now, while we spend the time, talking, laughing and really getting to know each other. I feel like I could tell him anything and I want to know everything about him too. Plus, there's all the time we've been spending together since he decided to take some time off from work. He makes me laugh and I feel happy just being around him. I feel like I've seen a much lighter side to him since he's taken more time away from his work, like when we were baking and he was joking around with me. Then of course, he has to go and save my life. I huff a humorless laugh, I'm going to miss him so much when he goes back to New York. I don't want him to go. My heart clenches tightly inside my chest and I wince at how much it hurts. I put my hand to my chest, attempting to calm my heartbeat and push away everything I'm feeling for him. He was just supposed to be my Christmas client, not someone I let myself fall for, but that's exactly what I've done. "He's leaving," I quietly remind myself.

I bend down and reach for the present I wrapped for Chris that I hid under the Christmas tree this morning. I pick it up and saunter over to the fireplace. I sit down in front of it, with a heavy sigh and set the present down beside me. I begin straightening the red bow on the small white, wire tree, bare of leaves or needles, just to do something to keep my hands busy. I don't want my present for him under the tree when everyone comes in to open presents. I want to be the one to give it to him and I'm not really sure I want anyone else to be around when I do. I want to be able to see his reaction. I hope he likes it. I hope it means as much to him as it does to me. I guess I want him to have it so he has something to remember me by when he leaves.

"There you are," Chris declares, as he strides into the room.

I have a quick intake of breath at the sound of his voice. My head snaps up to him and I smile shyly. "Hi," I greet him.

"Hi," he mumbles, returning my smile. He watches me as he crosses the room and sits down at the end of the love seat, near me.

"I was hoping you would come in before everyone else," I enlighten him. I fold my hands in my lap, a little nervous to give him his gift.

His smile grows with my comment. He clears his throat and informs me, "Yeah, they're walking around outside checking out all of the lights. It's truly a winter wonderland," he proclaims. "You did a great job," he praises.

I grimace, feeling as if I could've done more in the back, or maybe I could've handled my speech outside a little differently. I don't know. Maybe I shouldn't have done a speech at all. "Oh, I don't know," I mumble, uncomfortably.

His eyebrows draw down in confusion. "Merry, what's wrong?" he questions, his eyes full of concern.

I barely hesitate a moment, before I admit, "I feel like I made a fool out of myself outside, you know?" I prompt.

He shakes his head in denial and insists, "No, not at all." He pauses and tilts his head to the side as he stares intently at me, appearing slightly puzzled. "My mom totally believes that you're my girlfriend," he states. He pauses, assessing my reaction before he continues. "You really saved my skin there," he reveals, appreciatively.

I wince, but quickly try to hide it. "Oh. Yeah. I'm a great actress," I stammer. I force a smile on my face and look away as disappointment stabs at my heart, nearly overwhelming me.

"Oh, that reminds me," he asserts. He reaches into his pocket and pulls out a white envelope. "Here," he offers, holding it out to me.

I take it, cautiously. "What's this?" I probe.

I slip my pointer finger underneath the flap of the envelope and run it across the length, tearing it open. I reach in and pull out a small piece of paper and my heart instantly sinks to the pit of my stomach, at the sight of a check made out to me and signed by Chris. "It's your paycheck," he states. "You certainly earned it," he emphasizes.

I take a deep breath and exhale slowly, but I still struggle to catch my breath. I attempt to gulp down the lump in my throat. I have to say something, but I don't know what to say. If his comment about me pretending to be his girlfriend didn't confirm his feelings, handing me this check sure did. I know this is what we agreed to, but looking at this check hurts too much. This isn't what I want. I don't want to be paid to decorate his house or anything else for that matter. I want to have dinner together because he wants to spend time with me, not because he's trying something for an event. I thought he was enjoying our time together as much as I was, but I guess not. I force out a response and grumble, "Oh."

"Is something wrong?" he probes.

I look up and his eyebrows are drawn down in confusion at my reaction, which only makes it even hurt more. "Nope!" I answer. My whole body suddenly feels tense. "That's what this is, right?" I prod, not able to fight my grimace. "You're my boss and I'm your employee," I emphasize, feeling defensive.

His face falls, making me question my understanding of what he feels for me, yet again. "Oh. Well, I guess it is then," he mumbles.

My heart clenches painfully, but it doesn't matter. He's leaving. "I..." I begin, hesitating. I give myself a mental shake. I can't do this. "I think I need to get home," I finally blurt out. "You know, to feed Thaddeus," I add, giving him an excuse.

"Are you sure?" he prompts.

I pause, staring at him and trying to read his thoughts, but it doesn't help. I finally heave a sigh and nod my head. With a sad smile, I quietly concede, "Yeah, I'm sure."

I grasp the gift I was hiding from him behind my back and stand up. I walk up to him, sitting on the loveseat and force a smile as I hand him the gift. It's wrapped in gold wrapping paper and tied with a one-inch wide, royal blue ribbon, finished off with an elaborate bow on the top. I placed a blue and white snowman ornament on top and looped it through the ribbon to attach it to the box. "Here," I offer.

"What's this?" he questions, glancing up at me in surprise.

I paste a smile on my face, attempting to hide my pain, as I speak. "Just a little gift," I inform him. "You don't have to open it now if you don't want to," I add.

He starts to tear the wrapping paper off the gift almost instantly. He opens the box and stops with his mouth hanging open in shock, as he stares down at the present inside. It's a framed picture of Aunt Minnie Block's Chocolate Cream Pie recipe. I wanted to give him something to show we were connected before we ever even met, but I don't think it will have the same impact on him as it does on me. My stomach twists as I watch him. Of course I'm the one that had to fall for him. I knew better. I grimace and mumble, "Okay, well, goodnight." I turn slowly, the last of my hope disappearing as I trudge towards the front door.

I'm only a step away from the front closet to retrieve my coat, when Chris calls out, sounding desperate, "Meredith, wait!"

My stomach flips, as I spin around deliberately, tamping down my excitement, reminding myself I don't know what he wants. "What?" I prompt, barely able to maintain my balance. I cautiously walk back towards him.

He stands up and steps towards me. "Please don't leave," he begs. I look into his eyes and gasp at the pleading look in his eyes. "I don't know how it happened," he begins, "but somewhere along the way you became so much more than an event planner. You made

227

your way into my heart and I'm not about to let you go," he announces.

My heart begins to race. I take a deep breath and I look into his eyes, wanting this to be possible, but I have to attempt to be realistic. "Chris," I rasp, "it's not going to work," I insist, ignoring my heart trying to tell me it's breaking. "You're going back to New York..."

He instantly interrupts me, with a firm shake of his head. "I'm not," he declares, taking another step closer to me.

My heart pounds harder and I gasp for breath, as I hear almost nothing but the rapid flow of blood in my ears. "What?" I prod, my eyes wide and hopeful.

The corners of his mouth curve upwards, as he takes another step towards me. "I'm not," he repeats, with a small shake of his head. "I quit my job," he reveals. My mouth drops open and I gasp in shock. "I'm moving here, permanently," he proclaims, emphatically.

"I don't understand," I murmur, with a slight shake of my head. How can this be real? I need him to clarify.

"I'll tell you all about it tomorrow," he promises. "But for tonight," he begins, "please don't go," he pleads, urgently.

"I don't know," I mumble. I feel like this is all too good to be true.

He reaches for my hands and grasps them in his. The warmth of his touch sends tingles up my arms and down my spine. I don't ever want to let go. "Merry," he states my name, like a prayer on his lips and waits for me to meet his gaze. "This past month has been truly magical. I've never felt so sure about something, or someone, in my entire life," he emphasizes, his blue eyes sparkling. "You reminded me how important family is. You rearranged the priorities in my life. You made me want to be a better person," he asserts, emphatically.

"Really?" I prompt, overwhelmed by his admission. "I've fallen in love with you," he confesses. I gasp at his words, feeling as if this is a dream come true. My heart beats erratically as my whole body heats with love and hope. I open my mouth to respond to him, but he's not finished fighting for us. "You belong here, Meredith. You belong with me," he states, unequivocally. He gives my hands a squeeze, as he looks deep into my eyes, begging me to see the truth.

I feel it. The moment I realize that this is real and he's really not going anywhere. I pull my hands out of his and reach up, wrapping my hands around his neck. I tilt my head up towards him, my heart pounding so hard, that's all I can hear. A small smile touches his lips as he tips his head down towards me, meeting me halfway. We finally close the distance between us. His soft lips meet mine in a sweet kiss. He reaches up and cradles my face in his hands as he moves his lips tenderly over mine. I fall back on my heels with a happy sigh. I smile up at him, feeling so full of love, as he grins down at me. My heart beats erratically, while butterflies take over my insides. He's right. I know this is exactly where I'm supposed to be.

"I've fallen in love with you too," I admit, smiling up at him. He grins wide, his eyes never wavering from mine. I push up on my toes and press my lips to his, kissing him again, as he lovingly holds my face in his hands.

I hear the click of the front door, followed by excited chatter. I fall back on my heels, not able to wipe the smile off my face as I gaze into his eyes. He presses his forehead to mine, refusing to let me go and whispers, "Merry Christmas, Merry."

"Merry, Christmas, Chris," I reply, grinning up at him.

I slowly let my hands fall from around his neck. He lets one hand drop to his side, while he slides his other hand down my arm and entwines my fingers with his, clasping my hand tightly. Our family and friends begin to crowd into the room with us and find a seats around the room. Bella catches my eye and gives me a knowing look, smiling happily. I feel myself blush as I look back at Chris, still looking down at me with love and admiration.

We make our way to the love seat and sit down, hand in hand. He takes the frame I gave him and sets it on the table next to us. Then, he pulls our interlocked hands up to his lips and places a kiss on the back of my hand. He holds my gaze and rasps, "Thank you." I return his smile and sit back, leaning in close to his side, knowing he's thanking me for so much more than the gift. We both force ourselves to turn our focus to watching everyone else, as they begin opening presents, just enjoying being together. I never could've imagined my first Christmas client would not only bring a whole new meaning to Christmas for me, but he would also become the love of my life. Then again, I couldn't imagine it any other way.

The End

Acknowledgements

I would like to take this opportunity to thank everyone who has helped with this book. First, I would like to thank Alan Fogelman and Douglas C. Diana for investing in this Christmas movie. Without you, the movie or the book would never have come to be. Thank you to Producer, Amy Minter for all that you do! I always appreciate all of your support and encouragement! I, of course, need to thank my good friend, Candy Cain for asking me to collaborate with her once again on this Christmas movie (and book) project. This was such a beautiful location to spend our time working on this fun project! As always, I really enjoyed working with you and the food was a delicious bonus! Thank you again for asking me to be a part of this wonderful adventure.

I would like to thank Ashley Brinkman and Joe Kurak for bringing Merry and Chris to life in the film and on the pages. Thank you to Kenney Myers, Tara Westwood, Al Sapienza, Eliza Roberts, Robert Picardo, Catherine Mary Stewart, Deborah Rennard, Connie Shi, Julia Yorks, Austin Davis, Joseph Bessette, Allison Mullaney and the rest of the incredibly talented cast who helped bring life to some key characters of the story. It's so much fun to watch all of you work! I really enjoyed working with everyone in the cast and crew. So many of you have become like a family to me and I appreciate every one of you! Being able to watch the story come together on screen is something that's incredibly difficult to describe and for a writer, that's really saying something. I love being able to tell stories in all these different ways and watch them come to life.

Thank you to Heartly Creations for designing the beautiful paperback and digital book covers and of course to Gemelli Films for providing some of the images and bringing this story to life on-screen. It turned out incredible.

Thank you to Kelley and Nancy for all that you do and to all of my Beta Readers and fans for your support. I greatly appreciate all of your input and reviews. I value each and every one of you. Thank you, most of all, to my friends and family for their continuous support. I wouldn't be here without ALL of you. Plus, Allie, being able to work together on set, along with several friends was truly a gift for me! I love you all! And no matter what time of year it is when you read this, Merry Christmas!

Connect with the Author

For more Family Contemporary Romance, read more by Nicole Mullaney or Ethan Dulane. Connect with Nicole here:

Follow Me on Instagram
@nicolemullaney

Author Facebook Page
www.facebook.com/Nicole-Mullaney-Author-103006415283835/

BookBub
@NicoleMullaneyAuthor

For Adult Contemporary Romance, read books by Nikki A Lamers. Connect with her here:

Official Author Website
www.nikkialamersauthor.com

Author Facebook Page
www.facebook.com/pg/NikkiALamersAuthor

Follow Me on Instagram & BookBub
@NikkialamersAuthor

Author Goodreads Page

www.goodreads.com/author/show/8451774.Nikki_A_La mers

Amazon Author Page
https://www.amazon.com/Nikki-A.-Lamers/e/B00NU1VU8M

For more information on Gemelli Films, find them here:

Official Website
http://Gemellifilm.com/

Gemelli Films Facebook Page
https://m.facebook.com/GemelliFilms/

Gemelli Films Instagram Page
@gemellifilms

About the Author

Nicole Mullaney has always had a passion for reading and writing, especially romance. She grew up in Wisconsin with her sister and mom and dad. She always loved reading romance books and watching romance movies with her dad, something they both enjoyed. She now lives on Long Island in New York with her husband and two kids. She spends her free time reading or hanging out with friends and family.

She met Candy Cain through her daughter Allison's acting career. A few years later, at the end of 2018, she began collaborating with her on these film/book projects; Ivy & Mistletoe their first project together in this capacity. She enjoys being able to watch the stories come to life in different ways and be a part of it from the beginning.